YA both
2026

**NOVELS BY D.M. DE ALWIS**

A LION'S HEAD
A LION'S PRIDE
A MONKEY'S MASK - Forthcoming

# A Lion's Head

## By D.M. De Alwis

Copyright @ 2025 D.M. De Alwis

**A LION'S HEAD**
All rights reserved.

ISBN 978-1-0694018-7-8 (Paperback)
First Edition: 2025

Editing by Elise Abram of EMSA Publishing.
Cover design by D. Corlosquet.
Published by Ahasae Tharu Publishing, Toronto, Canada.

**AUTHOR'S NOTE:** While my work draws inspiration from characters from Buddhist/Hindu cosmology, this is a work of fiction. All of the characters, organizations, and events portrayed in this novel are either products of my imagination or are used fictitiously. To my South Asian readers for whom some characters hold great significance, my intention is to grow curiosity and understanding of our shared cultural heritage, histories, and dhamma.

For more information, visit **www.dmdealwis.com**

*For the storytellers who followed their muse to the end.*

Ettāvatā ca amhehi
Sambhatam puñña-sampadam
Sabbe devā (bhūtā, sattā) anumodantu
Sabba-sampatti-siddhiyā

Translation of Buddhist verse sharing blessings with all beings of the spirit realm:

*May all deities (ghosts, beings) share in those merits which are received for achieving success.*

God Mahabrahma is then born, who is alone. He longs for the presence of others, and the other gods are reborn as his ministers and companions. Eventually, one of the gods dies and is reborn as human, with the power to remember his previous life. This gives rise to the belief in a great creator.

- Buddhist Pali Canon

# 1

A strange duo clung to a cliff face high above the canyon, painted slate and grey by the setting sun. The first wore the head of a lion. His supernatural claws allowed him to scale the wall as though it were a tree. He looked more beast than man, his tail acting as a counterbalance as he reached for a ledge. From this distance, he stood two heads taller than the human climbing beside him—a length of rope connected them at their waists.

How Isha wished he could hear what they said.

The man-lion secured himself on the ledge and pulled the second man to relative safety. The human was ordinary. His grey leathers spoke of a military background. He carried no weapons. When his face turned sideways, Isha recognized his herdspeople's pronounced forehead and angled nose. Recognition reverberated a string of his blackened heart: Channa the younger, his once youthful deputy. He wore his hair braided in a protective topknot and still had his absurd thick mutton-chop sideburns, the relic of a childhood dare.

Channa slapped the man-lion's shoulder, reminiscent of old friends.

Envious, Isha imagined they enjoyed the exhilaration of hanging from the cliff. While he could see them in monochrome, he could not hear them. Here was the last warrior of his herd. Channa's ancient ancestor had *once upon a time,* called the Water Buffalo Gods, Isha and his wife, Chala, into existence. Channa had once stood faithful by Isha's side.

Isha's herdspeople had vanished with his wife around the time the man-lion had appeared.

Had this lion-headed construct of the gods supplanted him? As anger flared, Isha's energy ignited. The ground trembled. Channa was his. Channa was of the herd. He was the last.

Channa must be sent to the herd.

If only he knew where Chala had taken the herd.

Isha's vision broke. He covered his ears as if it could suppress the memory of her laughter.

Wherever she was, she was happy—without him.

He had been happy once, but now he was alone.

## A Lion's Head

*I've lost you forever.* Deep in his heart, too faint to hear, came the words, *It's all my fault.*

He stroked the soft, soothing braided necklace of human hair coiled around his neck with an idle finger. His attention returned to his lion-headed foe.

*It's all his fault.*

The man-lion's claws had pierced Isha's master's heart. That day, Isha had lost everything.

His wife and his herd . . . were gone.

The faraway, rational voice said. *It is my fault, my fault alone.*

The necklace coiled and constricted tighter. Isha deserved the pain. Fighting the yoke was futile. When Isha closed his eyes, he searched the blackness, trying to remember colour. He was sure it was still there. After a long pause, he gave in to the madness.

*It's all the man-lion's fault.*

Isha's vision formed again—reflected on the surface of the polished black stone. In it, the two climbers rested on a ledge overlooking a great chasm. Beneath them hurtled the white rapids of a tributary of the Ganga's waters. As if knowing he was being watched, the man-lion's face turned towards Isha. His gaze searched.

Isha froze. Could the man-lion reverse the spell and scry him?

This time, he released the vision on purpose. As the black and white scene faded, it revealed the polished stone mirror, and Isha's image reflected back at him. His black nose leather was wet. The sun danced shadows across his face, painting his snout and head in shades of black and grey. His once great horns were now twisted, yet they shone brilliantly white as they reflected the light. He looked into his fierce, commanding eyes.

*I am Maha Isha Sura*—the Great Water Buffalo. *I was created by the will of the people of my herd. I am Lord of the Animals and the First Minister to the God King.*

His humanoid body had once been more muscled and stocky than the man-lion's. His tail whipped in the wind. He snorted and glared.

*What am I now that my master, the King, is dead. My wife and my herd are gone.*

The braided coil around his throat squeezed, burning into Isha's hide, but not enough to choke him. The pain told him he was alive.

*I will be vengeance.*

## A Lion's Head

The man-lion would pay for destroying his world.

---

"He could have killed you." Sinha's deep baritone carried through to Channa's ears despite the bitter wind sweeping across the canyon. "I can't forgive him." The wind blew his heavy red mane into his eyes, obscuring his vision from time to time.

He had to get the words off his chest. They had spent hours talking about the seasons and the ways of the herd as if they were not on the trail of Maha Isha Sura, an errant god. Sinha could not understand Channa's fanatic devotion. Maybe understanding would alleviate his apprehension.

"My experience is not yours to forgive. I survived." Channa's voice held steady despite having clung to the cliff face for hours. "Life will kill you if you wait long enough."

"Maha Isha Sura left you for dead." Sinha's claws held them both secure.

The cliff was compacted soil, a deep brick colour punctuated by layers of clay, rock, and ash. So far, his claws had found purchase, though with every claw-hold he created debris.

Sinha hoped to reach the plateau before dusk. He looked up, relief sweeping over him. They were just below a short granite ledge. While he did not tire, his companion was mortal.

"I am of the herdspeople. Everything we do is for the herd." Channa shifted his weight between the rope at his waist and his grip. He blew on raw fingers before trying to get a handhold. Despite the loss in property, kicking off his boots had made Channa's ascent easier. He swung a leg, letting his toes find the ledge. His laughter betrayed both relief and desperation. The ledge would support their combined weight and provide him a respite. "I owe you a debt. The day you saved my life, Sinha, is the day you became part of my herd," he said.

Sinha chose not to retort with "A herd of one" as he pulled Channa's quivering, sweat and dust-laden body up the rest of the way.

Channa clapped Sinha's shoulder with one hand. "I know I am the last. I will restore Lord Isha to his senses." With his other hand, he fingered the greenish-black marble he wore hanging from the leather thong around his neck.

"This is why you are here," Sinha said despite his regret for bringing Channa on this mission. He would not tell Channa how his bull-headed god irked him.

Sinha laughed, hoping to lighten the mood. Maha Isha Sura's track had led them well into the canyon before collapsing beneath their feet. Had Sinha been alone, he would have jumped from the cliff. With Channa along, Sinha had been forced to find a humane way out of their predicament.

Sinha regretted choosing to go up. In hindsight, Channa could have survived a short fall into the rapids. A few broken bones and half-drowning would be a small price to pay for staying alive. He would have carried Channa to safety or lost him to the rapids.

He avoided looking down from the dizzying height, grateful for the solid ledge.

Would Channa's Lord Isha take pity on them? Sinha doubted he was the benevolent and protective god Channa described, but he had no proof. The few herdspeople he had met had not spoken about their god.

Not Channa. His faith bordered on fanatical. He believed himself responsible for his god.

An eerie sensation of being watched made the back of Sinha's neck itch. He looked out into the expanse—how could anyone see them? The shadows on the canyon walls were growing longer. The sun was descending. Ignoring the wind, he could hear the torrent of water raging below. The cloudless azure sky deepened in colour. How long did they have before the sun hit the horizon?

"Do you think he will listen?" Sinha asked, unaccustomed to Channa's long silence.

"I can make him listen. I will take him to our herd. None should be left behind."

"You know where Lady Chala took the herd?" Sinha asked. He had thought he knew everything there was to know about Channa. He knew all there was to know about his family: the herdspeople's customs, festivals, and everything a warrior needed to know about his gear. At no time had Channa hinted at returning to his herd, even when his mother, fellow warriors, and their beasts had been sent to the mortal realm for their safety.

"I do," Channa said. "The secret is in a riddle. Unsolved, the truth remains hidden. I both know and don't know where the herd is."

"A riddle. No hint?" he asked. Perhaps now was not the right time to joke. Channa's mother and his warriors would never reunite with Channa or the herd. They would die in the mortal realm and be reborn. Come to think of it, if the Lady Chala had taken the herd to the mortal realm, they would have died and been reborn many times over by now. That meant Channa's goal was to reunite Isha with his wife, Chala. He looked to his friend with renewed respect.

Sinha's next handhold failed. Sandy clay disintegrated, leaving him with a handful of dust. He scanned the rock from his left, up, and to the right, before making the mistake of looking down. The drop below was deep and dizzying. His claws might slow the fall, but their survival was not guaranteed. Fear stole the moisture from his throat. Channa would not know his fear.

The sun was close to the horizon. Could they wait there until dusk passed?

"Life is harsh, Sinha. Accept it. Predators, weather, and bad luck are constant. Lord Isha faced down the Asura King and was cursed. He made his choices to protect the herd. My father charged me to protect *him*, and I failed."

"How could you protect Lord Isha? You are just a human, and the Asura King was no friend to humans," Sinha growled. "Your Lord Isha had a choice."

Could Sinha dig a shallow tunnel in which to shelter? Or, better yet, dig upward a route to the surface. Channa would be protected from the wind and the terrifying elements of the immortal night.

"I admit. In the palace, I—we—were . . . ill-informed. I was blind to the truth until the King died." Channa's words slowed. "I was under a spell."

"You were under a coercive spell, yes. I remember," Sinha said. His efforts in digging had started to bear fruit. The upward burrow he dug appeared solid. The cliff showed no signs of deterioration.

"I will always support Lord Isha—" A loud rumbling from above interrupted Channa's words.

They both heard the bellow of a bull. The sound rang through the canyon. As it passed, the cliff became unstable. Sinha's sensitive footpads felt the shale tremble a warning. Solid ground began to turn to liquid under his feet. Instincts screaming, Sinha's toe claws locked down as the ground beneath them started to fall away.

"Landslide!" Sinha's roar was silenced by deafening thunder.

Channa slipped from the ledge; his outstretched hands grasped for Sinha's mane. He had nothing else to hold except the thick rope tied to their waists. The wall collapsed outwards in an explosion of rock and debris.

"Sinha," Channa whispered.

They both fell.

Sinha scrabbled to grab what remained of the cliff, relying on Channa's weakening grip to hold them together. Though Channa's weight jerked his head back, Sinha's strong muscles held them both secure. His fur provided little protection from the rain of sharp rocks. Bruised and seeing stars, he pushed through the concussive darkness.

Sinha leapt with inhuman strength from wherever he could get a foothold while striking his claws toward where the cliff had been.

Channa's grip failed, and Sinha felt the pull of the rope counter his leap, causing him to flip in mid-air. Nevertheless, four sets of claws found solid ground. He hung upside down, blood rushing to his head.

The ground shook. He bit his lip; the blood fuelled his determination. Rocks continued to rain, pelting his exposed arms and legs. Sinha's heart raced with fear. He bore the discomfort of knowing he would survive. Channa was the one exposed.

Life was unfair. Who was he to be the one to live when he had nothing and no one? Channa had a reason to live. Sinha should not have brought him along.

A deluge of water replaced the falling rocks. Sinha held both of them aloft as a century of stagnant rainwater flowed past, catching the last air from his lungs. Sinha gasped. He could not breathe. Invincibility did not give one a free pass from torture.

The waters joined the rapids and flooded the canyon far below. He could not look down to see how Channa had fared. Instead, he focused all his attention on holding on. The rope between them was taut until it wasn't.

"Channa!" he roared, catching a mouthful of water and gagging. He scrambled to cling to the crumbling cliff wall, soaked to the skin. Logic dictated his friend had fallen to his death. Channa's body would be carried away by the flood.

## A Lion's Head

Sinha fought to stay lucid as the world around him came to a standstill. He waited until the gathering immortal night was punctuated by the fierce winds and howling unseen spirits.

"Channa!" His hoarse bark echoed in the darkness. The violent dark wind stole his words and whipped tears from his eyes. He didn't know what he hoped for. How could a mortal human survive the drop?

"Channa, are you there?" he whispered. The wind wailed a lament.

Sinha fell. Before solid impact and ensuing darkness, he was comforted by a single thought: *I will live to see another day.*

As the blackness descended, he wondered why his instinct was to live.

# 2

**TEN YEARS EARLIER...**

"Reesho is dead," Channa the elder's voice boomed. A gong sounded nearby, summoning the Water Buffalo deities. Custom dictated the gong resound thrice before Isha and Chala could appear in the great hall.

Channa's voice was imbued with grief. The elder's aunt had spent her final years as the herd's chief shaman. She had been a young baby when their people had fled through the stargates escaping the destruction of the mortal realm. The refugees had a difficult life despite the safe haven populated by asura. Reesho had been the last of the herdspeople to have seen the stars and the moon in an open, earthly sky.

The vision of a rocky, arid terrain faded from Isha's scrying stone. He kept watch over their borders from the cool subterranean quarters he shared with his wife, Chala. As she awoke from her meditations, she murmured a low, slumber-filled moan about sweet grass, flies, and warm breezes. After a hundred years in the immortal realm, the equivalent of a thousand years in the mortal realm, Chala would not let go and move on. Their bond bore the strain from her bullish clinging to old ways. Perhaps, this time, if he agreed with her, they would come together.

"We took for granted the abundance of wild things, mud, flies, and dust," he said. *There, I have acknowledged her.*

"The mortal realm will always be our home, Isha. Just like our humans and heard beasts, we will never belong here, and now Reesho . . ." His wife's long eyelashes and half-closed amber eyes brimmed with unshed tears. She choked back a sob. Reesho had been her last living connection to the old realm.

"Take a moment, Chala. The gong has not sounded thrice."

A stream of tears ran down Chala's face.

He picked up an ornately brocaded towel, a relic from the days when they had worried the first crop of cotton would fail. Embracing his wife with one arm, he dabbed gently at her eyes. She wrapped her arms around him and held him. For a brief moment, they were one.

Her ears flicked as the gong sounded again, and she broke away from his embrace.

Channa the younger's clear alto replaced his father's. "Reesho is dead!"

"The younger Channa," Chala said, "he and his cousin, Davos—they are the last born. The gong has not been rung for any births since."

Isha sat down heavily on the side of the bed. The herd's decline: a yoke too heavy to bear.

"We must do something." She did not say, "or we will cease to exist." They would be forgotten.

The water buffalo herds had been domesticated by the time the first Channa had called them into being. In that dawn time, a cruder gong had rung three times, and a starved people had prayed. The eldest among them had stepped forward to sacrifice himself for the greater need. Before he could throw himself from the cliff, the black water buffalo-headed Isha and white bovine-headed Chala had appeared: a protector and a guardian to preserve against famine and extinction.

Channa the younger called the last summons. The gong rang for a third time. Isha and Chala walked out of their inner sanctum toward the great reception hall.

They strode through a maze of corridors to the great chamber underneath their home.

The inner sanctum held relics from the mortal world, a museum of artifacts brought during the first crossing: examples of flora and fauna, dead insects, and semi-precious stones. Their magic was most potent in the sanctuary, where the remains of their people and the lands they had left were stored. Nothing decayed in the immortal realm.

If they were home, this would have been a lush green field under a sky full of stars. When they had arrived in the realm, Isha discovered he could manipulate the four elements: earth, wind, fire, and water. Chala's gifts were far more curious—control over aether and time, which she used in good measure to speed fertility cycles.

Isha willed the thousands of zirconia stones embedded in the ceiling to illuminate. Looking up meant seeing the stars as they existed in their home during the summer solstice. He had not found a suitable replica for the moon.

Men and women carried amber torches to light the way. The herdspeople had assimilated over many generations. Fire starters were crafted with the help of the asura, the divine beings native to the immortal realm.

Seeing the torches brought Isha's mind to the world outside the herdlands. The greater population of asura had crowded into overflowing cities while more human migrants, brought to the realm by the Greater Gods, had founded hundreds of remote settlements. Isha's people had profited from the growing asura dependence on human handiwork and food.

Having said their farewells, Reesho's body had been wrapped in a plain shroud. A dozen or more of her kin accompanied the body. No matter how much time had passed, each death was hard to bear. Isha had bounced her on his knee as a toddler. As an adult, she had charmed him with her songs and impressed him with her conduct. Reesho the elder had berated him when he had been lax with their needs.

"Lord Isha, Lady Chala—our respects to you and to our late shaman Reesho," the younger Channa said. "We bring her body to you to release her into the next life."

Careful of where they stepped, two men set the stretcher down in the middle of a circle filled with the grey-white ashes of their long-dead ancestors. Isha and Chala took their places at Reesho's head and foot.

## A Lion's Head

Corporal forms were eternal—her remains required magic to break down and release the spirit trapped within. From there, her past actions, or karma, would lead her to her next evolution. While human rebirth was preferred, many in the past had chosen to return as a herd beast out of love and loyalty, providing precious manure and nutrition.

"Let us guide her spirit back to our herd," Chala intoned. She closed her eyes to accompany Reesho's spirit into the afterlife. While Chala often served as a guide, Shaman Reesho had practiced the old ways and would know her path.

"Think of her and remember her life. Your memories will draw her. She will come home."

But would Reesho's spirit choose her descendant's womb? Isha had never worried about such things before. This was Chala's domain. Reesho's husband had reincarnated into a calf that had followed behind her for two years before each had forgotten the bonds that tied one to the other.

He was one with Chala. They were one. He caught the subtle flick of Chala's ears, an excited quiver in her tail as she was filled with intense rapture. He waited for her to raise her hands to symbolize Reesho's departure.

Instead, she sang an old herder's tune, a lullaby, one he had not heard in over a hundred years. Perhaps it was the song Reesho had remembered as her body died. The spirit trapped within the body was held in stasis by the deceased's last thoughts, the memory of a song. The song called the sun to chase the moon, to grow the meadow flowers, and turn the seasons.

"Reesho goes to the . . . the mortal realm. I see. She goes to a womb. People—our people—gather to pray for us to come home to them. She is in the womb of a shaman mother versed in our ways. Reesho will be a prophet to our people. She will guide us back to our home." Chala opened her eyes with a gasp.

She was met with silence and disbelieving stares. Only Channa the elder and his wife smiled with relief and prostrated themselves on the ground. Others followed their motion.

Hope was absent in the fearful looks exchanged between the young. Led by Channa the younger and his uncle Oumo, they shuffled their feet and whispered the question, "What will this mean for us?" Were they so assimilated that the mortal realm had become a myth?

Isha inspected the body to ensure nothing of Reesho's spirit remained. He dared not begin the next stage without making sure the body was cold, the fluids had stilled, and no breath remained. Invisible hands raised the body into the air. He called on fire to consume the corpse. There was no noxious smell, no smoke, no fuel except the flesh. A small cloud of ash remained. The invisible hands let go. The ash drifted down, falling like snow to join the ashes of her long-dead husband, children, parents, and friends.

Her eldest living son, Oumo, approached.

"Oumo, son of Reesho, your beloved mother is gone. She will be remembered as mother, grandmother, and shaman of our herd," Isha said. "She will find welcome and prosperity in the next life."

"Thank you, Lord Isha." Oumo bowed low.

"You are now the eldest of your clan," Isha said as the significance of Chala's words dawned on him. Oumo and his wife Saida did not have children, though she was in her child-bearing years. If the conditions were right, Reesho could have entered Saida or another relative's womb. *Reesho has passed to the mortal realm. Dare I believe we will also find our way back home?* Isha held his breath. *After all this time, what is hope?* For the first time in a century, his wife sat by his side, emanating contentment. *How I wish I could believe it to be true.*

Drums and flutes played as Reesho's clan circled their deities and danced to the beat. Slow, at first. As the pace quickened, the elders stood to the side. The children danced, hopping from one foot to another, chanting, yipping, and grunting. His long life meant Isha's time passed slowly relative to the aging human population. *How did I fail to notice our youngest, Davos, is in his teens? Where are the babies, toddlers, and children? Chala is right to worry.*

As the extended clans arrived to join the wake, Isha counted the children. They numbered no more than a dozen in a sea of hundreds, all of an age to marry and have children, and yet, there were few who wished to partner. Fewer who wished to bring children to life.

He felt a lump stick in his throat as he and Chala were invited to complete the final dance. His magic provided fertile earth, not fertile bodies. Chala's magic was more attuned to the heart and mind. With their population in decline, Chala and Isha's powers were also in decline—couldn't she increase the herd's reproductivity? Her obsession with the mortal realm had distracted her from the needs of their herd.

"That's not how it works," was what she would say when asked. He had stopped asking.

Their bitter reality included the growing population of asura who did not want humans in their realm. All the more reason to find a way back to the mortal realm.

Fear caught in Isha's throat. Those other human settlements depended on absentee gods and their faith in the Greater Gods to save them. From all accounts, the Greater Gods were doing a terrible job of looking after their humans—what good would they do his herd?

Isha sat in meditation after the festivities. Mindful of his need to ruminate, Chala left him alone. From beneath the cool ash of the circle, the black earthstone underneath hummed.

Isha dug his hand into the ash, touching the earthstone. The great slab of obsidian hummed louder with his touch. What did it mean? This was a piece of the mortal realm—earth—which he had carried through the stargate. When their population had been ten times greater, he had been twice his size and height. Today, a hundred years later, he only stood a head taller than his tallest warrior—he could not lift the rock without magic.

His spell raised the ash to the ceiling of the cavern, leaving the large polished black rock exposed. The humming grew louder—did it vibrate?

"Isha, what are you doing?" Chala had returned, startling him. She stared at the cloud of ash hanging in mid-air. "So many people. A hundred years of memories, preserved in ash for eternity."

He told her about the humming rock. With reverence, he replaced the ash in its hearth. They sat vigil, expecting something to happen.

Nothing did.

As night receded, Isha walked out into the cool dawn's light rather than weather a stormy discussion with Chala. She remained behind, watching the rock with the patience of a mother. Maybe the rock would give up its secrets to her.

## A Lion's Head

Fifty years ago, he had agreed to find a way back home. He could not bear to tell Chala how he had been humiliated while petitioning for their return—forced to grovel at the feet of the minor asura lords—only to be turned away. As a deity created by mortals, Isha shared his form with a beast of burden. The pompous man-faced elite shunned and derided him. Depleted, he returned to the herdlands to build their defensive borders.

Listening to the Greater Gods had brought him to the immortal realm. His people had been abandoned. He could not bring himself to call on the Greater Gods for help. Not while angry and resentful.

Chala was right to set her focus on finding a way home. She was always right.

He walked out of the domed stone building and surveyed the yurts and tents. It had all been one vast plain when they had first settled. Over time, they had developed ways to grow and harvest what had once been gathered. The plain was now rolling farmlands. With no seasons, they cycled the crops. Even the asura populace sought after the fruits of their labours.

The herdspeople established caravans and fixed trade routes between scattered human colonies. There were the traders peddling food via the caravans, the herders, and the craftspeople. Above all, the storytellers, shamans, and musicians were valued for keeping records of the passing of time.

As he rounded the training grounds, the two youths from Reesho's funeral caught his eye. Both were thickset, chiselled specimens of his people. They carried the seeds of their father and grandfathers who had come before them. Davos and Channa were of good stock. One convention persisted: every generation produced a "Channa" who would inherit the role of chieftain.

"Channa the younger and your cousin Davos? When did you grow old enough to wield axes?" Isha asked, repeating the jest he had begun in childhood.

They bowed in return. The younger Channa held out cupped hands, dropping to one knee to make an offering. Isha accepted the small clay amulet depicting a bull's head.

"You're getting better, I will add this to my collection," he said, pocketing the token, delighted to receive the unexpected gift.

He waved for them to continue. Under scrutiny, Channa performed well. The memory of Channa's past lives interwove with images of countless men overlaying the youth. Isha had seen all but one of their lives. Standing before him, wielding an axe, was the same ancestor who had called him and Chala into being. He owed this Channa his existence.

Davos, on the other hand, seemed nervous. Three times he missed his mark. He carried a younger soul, one easily frustrated by the nuances of life.

Isha was not surprised when Davos threw down the axe and declared, "I will never be a warrior. I am not as good as Channa." He kicked a stone with his foot. For some, shedding childhood was difficult.

"There are many levels of success, Davos. You do not need to run to ride," Isha offered.

"Lord Isha, I am too weak," Davos said. The boy had developed a habit of impressing through his failures.

His cousin cuffed him. "Why would you say that to Lord Isha?" Channa hissed.

"Practice, Davos. Persevere. You will become stronger. Every member of this tribe is valued for what they contribute. You will find your way," Isha said. Leaving the boys to continue their practice, he continued on his walk.

These events had played out many times before. He needed to discuss the matter with

Chala. The boy's ego would benefit from separating him from his shining warrior of a cousin. Perhaps, he could solve the mystery of the stargates.

Lord Surya, God of the Sun, had led the herdspeople through a shallow tunnel in the side of Mount Tipila. After thousands of beasts, men, women, and children—carrying all that they owned—had flooded through the tunnel, it had flashed golden and both the god and tunnel had disappeared.

Had Isha known they would be trapped in the immortal realm for generations, he would have refused the call of the Greater Gods. Perhaps his people would have found another way to survive.

Yes, Davos could join those sent to search for the stargates. Maybe if they went farther, to the outer reaches—

His thoughts were interrupted by a commotion. From where he stood, he saw a rising charcoal cloud of dust headed toward him. From its midst, the runner and his beast, wet from the exertion, were painted black. It stuck to their sides, making them look like an animated stone chess piece in play. No one should run that fast and risk foundering.

## A Lion's Head

Isha sent a silent summons to the rest of his hunters and warriors. The herdlands were secured by an impenetrable canyon of his making. The land he had sculpted spoke to him of the nauseating trespassers and their ill intent.

"Lord Isha, an invading army approaches," the runner shouted from his mare.

"They need not come any closer. Let's ride out to meet them and find out what this is about," he answered. He bellowed a deep, resonant grunt—echoed by the herd beasts—calling his warriors to his side. Mounted on lithe horses bred to manoeuvre around stampeding buffalo, hundreds of men and women, heeding the call of the warrior, streamed from all directions and raced to his side.

"Let my Lady know what is happening," he told the runner whose mare looked as if it needed to rest. "Go easy. At a walk."

His hunters whooped and screamed shrill war cries, a massive cloud of black dust rising in their wake. There was joy in the charge. He ran at their head, flying across the landscape like a murmuration of birds.

As always, Chala was right; in truth, they were no warriors. The herdspeople had never known war. This generation were lambs, never having blooded their knives with the flesh of man.

His party reached the rise of a hill past the lookout tower and fell silent. An armed force extended across the horizon in all directions, on the other side of their canyon border. asura, men, demons, mortals and strange beasts as far as the eye could see. Was it a trick of magic or the talent of a god?

Isha detected no sorcery.

The soldiers parted like a river, creating a pathway for their leader, a giant dark-haired asura, to walk toward him.

Was it some sort of powerful mind control?

Isha was immune. The magic failed to find purchase.

His hunters were outnumbered. Only the canyon and his ability to collapse the ground or its walls stood between the asura and his conquering of the herdlands. Isha could not kill so many. He was not that type of god. He could trap them, but for how long? Where would his herd escape to if the enemy took to the air?

Where were the Greater Gods?

Isha looked to the sky, hoping for their sudden appearance.

## A Lion's Head

*You bring us to these lands but fail to protect us!*

The great asura stood at about Isha's height. His thick moustache hid the source of his long, curved yaksha fangs, which ended below his chin. He wore ochre-coloured robes brocaded in gold.

For a time, they stared at each other. Neither spoke. The great army stared down Isha's tiny band of warriors, who fidgeted with discomfort.

"Who are you?" Isha asked.

The Yaksha smiled.

His smile was captivating.

Isha could not help but return a smile. His hunters relaxed. With enough time, they would step forward, forgetting their past to willingly join the horde. Isha would need to think fast.

"You don't leave your lands, do you, bull-headed ... man?" the asura asked Isha.

"I see no reason to when my people are here," Isha replied.

"The gods have forgotten their mortals here." Contempt marked the Yaksha's words.

"The Greater Gods are the reason we are here, but I speak for these mortals," Isha said.

"These people do not worship those gods?"

"They do not."

"Yet, they worship you?"

"Yes."

"You ... are a god?"

"That is the way of our people," Isha said.

"I am called Hiranyakshipu—or you might know me as the golden-robed victor," the asura said. When Isha did not react, he continued. "Join me in changing the order of the universe."

"Why would I join you? Your kind destroyed our realm," Isha said.

"A boar-faced man killed my brother; consider us even." Hiranyakshipu's brows furrowed as his eyes narrowed. His rage smouldered until he shook his head, resuming an expression of feigned gravitas.

"He is no relation of mine," Isha said with an equal measure of rage. The asura never failed to think of him in league with the vilified Varaha, the boar-faced killer of the last king. He had weathered enough derogatory taunts.

"I inherited his kingdom and I have conquered this realm, I hold dominion over all asura, humans, and demons," Hiranyakshipu said. His arms spread wide, marking the silent horde.

"How is that possible?"

"Simple. I can not be defeated. I will show you. Join my forces."

"And if I don't?"

"Join or be assimilated," Hiranyakshipu replied. His ivory teeth and fangs gleamed.

Isha wondered if the King could hold sway over him. He belonged to his herd and the mortal realm. Could the immortal's spell hold him as it would a mortal? The legions of asura, men, demons, and weird beasts stood in formation covering the barren hills for as far as he could see. His herd sense could distinguish between followers and the mindless. Those not under the asura's spell shifted their weight as they stood, the minute movements catching his eye.

"Do I get some time to think about my choices here?" Isha asked. He scratched an ear. He could send word to Chala to take the remaining herd and flee, but where would they go? The Greater Gods were absent. There was no stargate to take them away from here. What might he do to leverage his herd? Isha swept his gaze across the army, lingering on the empty wagons.

Empty wagons . . .

Provisions!

The King's army, at least the humans and their beasts, needed food and supplies.

"Provisions," he said.

"What?" Hiranyakshipu blinked.

"I can provide your army with provisions. Our lands produce bountiful harvests. We are known for providing goods across the realm. Let me provision your army." Isha rose to his full height and waved at the expansive lands behind him. "My humans and our lands, stay out of your war with the gods. In return, we provide your provisions, and my herd remains intact."

"What is the price for your loyalty?"

"Stargates," Isha replied.

"What?" Hiranyakshipu blinked again.

"You give my herd a route back to our home realm. Give us access to the stargates."

"We have yet to find them," Hiranyakshipu muttered, caught off guard.

"I am sure you will. You have a large army. Someone will find them. When you do, I want my herd returned to our home realm." Isha stood with his hands on his hips. A water buffalo stands its ground. Water buffalo protect their territory and herd. He held the upper hand. Provisioning a sizeable army was no

## A Lion's Head

mean feat. His rare ability to make lands prosperous would be hard to match.

Hiranyakshipu looked at the canyon. "You did this?" he asked.

"I did."

"What else do you want?" The fanged asura gazed at Isha with newfound respect.

Isha bristled. Hiranyakshipu had conquered the realm without harming anyone. He had already secured all he needed. Curiosity paired with hungry ambition drew the words from him. "A title and status . . . under your leadership, of course," Isha replied.

"You are called?"

"Isha Sura"

"Done, Maha Isha Sura, you may be my first minister," intoned the asura, "and lord of the animals."

"Maha?" Isha asked.

"What we have negotiated here today is great—*maha*."

"Hiranyakshipu, I accept," announced Isha. He bowed low, his hunters following his lead. As one, the army and the King bowed in response.

# 3

**ONE YEAR LATER...**

Though her expression remained stoic, Isha recognized the sadness and regret behind Chala's thick eyelashes. Her plain ivory white suit suggested she mourned. They were one—he knew she was missing him.

The last time he had been home to see his wife, she had redecorated the quarters they no longer shared. Her gown had been the restful green reminiscent of the river marshes, ornate with brown embroidered leaves and dark beads at the hems, lines, and high collar. His tan, rust, and brown robes were sewn together from leaf-shaped patches—an ode to an autumn its makers had never experienced.

"Must the walls be green? Pasture of my heart, don't get me wrong, I think it's nice, but I start to get hungry for sweet grass or fresh meadow flowers while staring at this wall." Isha Sura wondered how to turn her obsession around. She had inscribed an almost invisible riddle into the wall. Green lettering on a green background. A secret message only they could read:

*Home is where lies the sweet grass.*
*To the plains and the harvest moon;*
*Look to the green moss.*
*You will be home soon.*

He ran a finger over the characters. We *will be home soon.*

"Don't look at the walls, Isha. Look at me. When the burden is too heavy, at least we have each other," Chala replied.

The bottom of Isha's stomach dropped with the excitement of delight and desire. His wife's long eyelashes and half-closed amber eyes brimmed with affection for him.

"Looking at you reminds me of home—our real home," she continued.

"My scruffy imperfections remind you of home?" He embraced her. How did she manage to smell like sweet grass?

"You are my safe space. Will you be home again?" She tortured him with her heartache. His chest tightened.

"I have my duties. Our people grow vegetables; the God King gives them allowance to roam," Isha said.

"You would have them be farmers and merchants?" Her truth stung. Yet, he had raised the value of his people above that of other humans, protecting them from their asura overlords.

"We must adapt, or we will have nothing," he replied, searching her face for a sign that she understood. Seeing only her pursed lips, he regretted his words. There was no way back. He sat, the stuffed cotton pouf holding its shape under his weight. "The stargates remain hidden, but the God King will find them."

"You and your Asura King turn your back on the Greater Gods!" Chala's rage burned hot and pure.

Let her resent him. She had not seen what he had seen. She did not know what he knew. How could she understand? At all costs, he would protect her. He was one with her. "Chala, there is nothing we can do," he said. "We chose to come here. The they led us here, only to abandon us."

Worse than rage, a mask of stoicism descended over Chala's face, an attempt to hide her resentment of him. They were one. No matter how she masked herself, he could feel her.

They were connected through the herd. He sent her his love along the bond.

She smiled back, sheepishly. The storm cloud lifted.

*We are forever one.*

Her hands touched his. He inhaled her scent and flicked his ears. Their horns grazed, teasing heart-pumping intimacy.

She smiled. Under her gaze, he forgot his failings. She understood his intention to protect.

They were a perfect pair: she, a beautiful white, bovine-headed woman; he, a well-muscled, black, water buffalo-headed man. The doorways in their dwelling were built as wide as they were tall to accommodate his great horns. His sorcery kept their fields fertile and prosperous. Her magic healed and gave knowledge of the beyond. Through the mortals, they represented a connection to the sacred earth and the life-giving water in their home realm.

They would find a way home.

**FOUR YEARS LATER...**

Four years had passed since he had agreed to be the King's first minister. Isha sent secret messages to his people between the lines of the God King's demands. He scried the brown messenger peahen's oration through his polished black obsidian stone as it ended with gasps from the assembled elders of the herd. The new mandate had increased the God King's share of the harvest. Human settlements would go hungry.

Chala invited the council to speak. The elder Channa's hands danced as he spoke on behalf of Isha. He had rehearsed his speech—the rhetoric of avoiding conscription and gaining safe passage by keeping the Asura King happy was met with a chorus of grumbling.

"We cannot stand by while others suffer," Oumo said.

"We cannot, and yet we must survive this storm. And a storm it is. One in a series of such storms," Chala said. "Lord Isha is not in a position to contradict the King's orders." Her gaze silenced objections.

"Then, what good is he?" a discordant voice called out.

Isha could not make out the speaker. His vision had faded to greyscale, and the ringing in his ears warned he was being watched . . . again.

*I am the King's hostage.*

## A Lion's Head

He had failed Chala and his people. He lowered his heavy head onto his tired hands and stared at his reflection in the small polished stone. He wanted to be with them, to be free to express his anger. He cursed his ambition.

His people had thrived in the first year under the Hiranyakshipu's dominion. Far-reaching human settlements had welcomed their traders. He and Chala had been excited, anticipating news of a stargate.

He had thought nothing of the summons to settle the last terms of his agreement. He had not seen the enclosure until the gates slammed shut. He was foolish. Chala was right; he was in no position to disagree with the God King.

Isha had played a dangerous game with Hiranyakshipu and lost. He blew out the vision, shook his head to clear the pressure between his ears, covered the polished stone with a cloth and assessed his lonely domain. He had lived in these empty rooms alone for almost four years. The hard chair upon which he sat. A small, unadorned table for his scrying stone. An ornate chest contained the offerings of food that were replenished as often as his herd traders passed through the city. A seldom-used lattice bed, complete with a soft mattress, cushions, and pillows. His tower room looked out on an empty court. The vacant rooms below were designed to house his servants and men. His rooms were as sparse as the day he had arrived.

There was no home without the herd.

He did not trust the palace servants, human though they may be. They wore the hypnotic look of those under the God King's geas. He dared not bring his people here. How could he call himself Lord of the Animals? He was created by the herdspeople to be Lord of the Herd. *Foolish water buffalo—why did you crave recognition from outside your herd?*

The walls were a nausea-inducing grey—not that it mattered. She would never see the walls. Chala was wise in her refusal to leave the herdlands. He should have been so wise.

Hiranyakshipu reigned as an autocrat, and Isha's role as spokesperson went against his nature. The asura had welcomed him upon arrival, supporting the King's war against the Greater Gods. The asura of the court knew he held no real power. He was Hiranyakshipu's stooge, representing the King's interests.

Meanwhile, Chala had assumed Isha's role in the herd. She spoke on behalf of the herdlands. These days, she spoke on behalf of the greater human population. They would have no representation otherwise.

He was a puppet. The King's policies on mortals within the immortal realm made him sick. What *was* Hiranyakshipu's weakness?

He suppressed the thought. Isha's ability to manipulate matter was of no use here. There was a presence watching him. The ringing in his ears grew louder. Ambition had yoked him to the King's service. Pulling his weight kept the King's armies from sweeping through the herdlands. The herd was safe, but he was a hostage in the capital, guaranteeing Chala's compliance.

Did Hiranyakshipu suspect he was one with his wife? He trusted Chala to satisfy the God King's requests. She would know how to rescue the people in the settlements. In his way, he rebelled against his bonds. His warning would give the people time to escape starvation, enslavement, and, worst of all, forced conscription to the soulless army.

*My Chala—take the people into the herd. When we find the stargates, everyone will be free.*

Hiranyakshipu feared the Greater Gods would raise an army against him. He had tasked Isha to create a physically inhospitable barrier around his capital. Using his gift of manipulating earth and water, Isha had spent several years rebalancing the water tables and trading fertile and arid zones. Now, a single heavily guarded route led in and out of the capital.

Isha was of the water buffalo. Physically and mentally, his skin was thick. He used it to resist bullishly, playing politics and feigning friendship. No one would suspect him of rebellion. There were ways through the barrier. He trusted the all-knowing gods to find their way.

A bell rang three times—Isha was being summoned. He pulled on his sombre black robes of state and left his rooms, a giant shadow moving in the darkness of the quiet night. His ears itched for the sound of people or night creatures. He paused for a brief moment to look up at the darkness of the sky. With over a thousand years to recover from Armageddon, surely, night in the mortal world would sing with a chorus of birds, insects and animals as before. He joined a throng of asura headed towards dancing orange and yellow lights projecting from the great courtyard and the festival of fire dedicated to Holika, the King's sister.

A great bonfire burned high in contrast to the pitch black of the night sky. Isha blinked, blinded by the light. He made out Holika's tall and rotund silhouette against the flames. She wore a multitude of gauzy colourful robes and scarves of every hue that twirled as she danced both in and out of the flames. Every now and then, she would hurl a scarf into the fire, and it—leaving her possession—would burst into flame, creating a burst of coloured ash that floated up on the wind to dust the crowd of awed spectators. Through millennia of study, Holika had become impervious to heat and fire. Tonight, she had promised a spectacle to entertain an assembly of the King's supporters.

Entertainment that delighted in excess: such were the whims of the immortals. Isha would have preferred a cacophony of drums, the whir of human dancers, and the songs of the storytellers. Instead, the flames and crowd roared, the heat kept the crowds back, and Holika danced.

He stood by the royal family as was expected of his rank. Hiranyakshipu appeared no older than his sons. Different rules of longevity applied to asura. They attested to having an unbroken line of ancestors despite not reproducing in the messy way of humans.

Since aging and death were inevitable—occurring as an onset of general decline or a dissolution of form towards the end of an asura's life—the fear of death, or a lost legacy, led many to seek favours from higher beings.

Isha had no ancestry or descendants, only Chala, his wife. He would have been pleased to have had a child. Perhaps, his herd were his children. He felt a pang of envy seeing all six of the King's sons in attendance. The motley crew of young men bore their father's robust features and fangs. Each had grown to different heights and presented themselves in varying tones of light to dark skin. He had only interacted with the astute Bashkala, who served as a herald to his father.

The theme of the night was fire as a purifying agent. Hiranyakshipu walked with his sister over fire-damped coals. The flames roared back into life. The fire would burn off the sins of his sons, blessing the next generation. Holika would protect them as she carried each man over the flames. A doting aunt, her love for her nephews and nieces preceded her.

## A Lion's Head

Bashkala, the youngest, went first. With nothing to fear, he cheered when set safely down on the other side. Next, Shibi and Hlada were carried in her arms as she twirled and danced in the flames. Sweat beaded their faces.

She carried the larger Anuhlada on her back. He waved his hands but failed to look comfortable as his white sleeves turned black from the flames.

Samhlada lacked enthusiasm for the ordeal, but Hollika danced, giving him time to steady his nerves.

Isha watched the King, Hiranyakshipu, who had an arm around his eldest, Prahlada.

Crown Prince Prahlada's intense devotion lay with the Greater Gods. His supporters were in open rebellion against the King's rule. Like Isha, the Prince was a hostage. Isha had not been at the palace long enough to witness the King's rumoured attempts at filicide. What he saw was a father frustrated with his obstinate son; Prahlada would not be swayed from his faith.

"Holika's fire will burn away your sins of disobedience once and for all, my son," Hiranyakshipu said.

"As you wish, Father," Prahlada replied.

Out of caution, Isha kept his distance. Seeing the King's sons brought the faces of his own to mind. He was father to three young bulls and knew the sometimes complicated relationship between father and son well.

Isha's instincts sharpened as Holika, the giantess, approached. Her dread-filled gaze locked with the King's. Hiranyakshipu gave her a slight nod, and ushered Prahlada towards the fire.

"I trust you," the Prince said with open arms and a smile of welcome. Holika gathered him in her arms and carried him like a small child into the flames. She sat with him cradled in her lap as the crowd roared with excitement. Isha noted those who cheered for Prahlada and those who jeered for Prahlada's demise.

Though the pyre's heat intensified, the King called for more fuel. The crowd surged back from the heat. Flames reached for the heavens, touching the sky. The festival of light took on hues of blue, black, and every shade of gold.

Blinded, Isha turned away and caught Hiranyakshipu's whisper, "Hollika, it is time," despite the crackle of fuel and the roar of the flame.

## A Lion's Head

Isha stepped back from the unbearable heat.

The world slowed as Hollika let the Prince fall from her lap. She stood behind him, her face a cloud of regret.

A sadistic grin formed on Hiranyakshipu's face as fire enveloped his eldest son. The Prince's brothers and mother shouted desperately. Cries of anguish and screams came from the watchers.

The gathered asura went mad. A sadistic few spurred the flames higher. Others, including Isha, called on their magic to extinguish the fire.

Prahlada stood, enveloped by fire. His eyes closed, his lips moved in silent prayer.

Holika's scream carried across, silencing the crowd. Her horror was heard as much as it was felt. Her robes and body took flame. She projected her pain.

Isha crumpled to the floor, feeling his skin burn. She burned, and the crowd writhed with her pain.

Unscathed and unaware of his aunt's fate, the statuesque Prahlada stood in reverie while surrounded by the roaring fire. When, at last, he turned to face Hollika—a look of horror—as he grasped the situation and reached out, too late to save her.

The last of Hollika's corpse collapsed into the fire. Her body turned to ash. Silence descended on those who had fallen to the ground screaming before they lost consciousness.

"Are you satisfied, father?" Prahlada said, turning to face Hiranyakshipu.

Hollika's remains had vanished into the inferno, and Isha was freed. His ears filled with the noise of panicking asura and the out-of-control pyre. He had fought an unseen force that blocked his attempt to extinguish the blaze. He was not the only one.

Rain began to fall. Wind damped the flames, choking the air feeding the pyre. Holika's ashes, swept up in the melee, began to rain over the crowd. The dust bore every colour she had worn.

The water and ash painted everyone in every colour. The ashes were her legacy.

Isha returned to his quarters more homesick than when he had left. He sat in stunned silence until dawn emerged.

At daybreak, servants spread sand to bury the scorched earth. The palace halls were empty. Someone had blocked the spring feeding the bathing pools, leaving them polluted with ash. The pools would take days to run clean. Holika had been well-loved. Her remains lingered as a reminder to Hiranyakshipu.

Isha cleaned himself as best he could pulling water from an underground spring. He then attended the King at his breakfast.

Hiranyaksha appeared nonplussed by the loss of his sister. Seeing Isha's questioning look, he responded, "Fire purges sin. Holika burned for her sins. She deserved her fate." The King's plate was piled high with meat and flatbreads.

Holika must have regretted her role in endangering Prahlada's life.

Although the table was set with an assortment of fruits, vegetables, and grains, Isha could not stomach any of it. He glanced over at the man who had others commit sins in his stead.

The God King was not one to feel remorse. He ate with gusto. "I spent the early part of my life earning my invincibility. How is it that *he* has done nothing to earn a boon—but can not be harmed?" Hiranyakshipu said.

"I am not used to your customs," Isha replied. "Can it be that he inherited his invincibility from you?"

"Impossible . . . though maybe you are right. I will think about this."

Hiranyakshipu called for servants to wash his hands and face. More servants removed the dishes from which he had been eating and returned with trays of cakes and sweets.

"We asura never had any desire for food until the humans arrived. I must say, I will miss it," Hiranyakshipu said. The one-sided conversation continued with Isha nodding and providing monosyllabic answers as the King talked about the size of the crowd that had gathered and how silly his larger-bodied sons had looked being carried by Holika. The King chortled and slapped the table.

"Sire, I am reminded—the time has passed for me to return to the herdlands," Isha said. "Seeing all of your family together has me missing my home."

"I am unkind for keeping you for so long, Isha," Hiranyakshipu said, with a menacing gleam in his eyes. "Do you give up your position as first minister?"

"Bashkala will be happy to fill in for me while I am gone."

## A Lion's Head

"I had a thought on the human problem: send the humans to their next lives, surely they will be reborn in the mortal realm." The King stabbed a morsel of venison.

"It is an option," Isha said. He did not have it in him to argue. Hiranyakshipu was right: humans were animals. They did not belong in the immortal realm. *He* did not belong in the immortal realm either.

The King looked up from his meal to meet Isha's gaze. "I fear you have been away too long, Isha. Do you fear your wife and herd will cast you out?"

"I hope not, Sire." At the King's mercy, Isha looked away.

Hiranyakshipu chuckled. The chuckle grew into a laugh. "Bring your men here to train with my finest."

"They are human and unwelcome in the capital," Isha replied.

"I will equip them for their return to the mortal world," Hiranyakshipu said. "Who knows what kind of life your herd will encounter after they cross the threshold?"

"I will think on it." Isha said.

"I am sorry to have kept you here for so long. Go home, dear friend."

"Thank you, Sire," he said.

Alone and running the secret paths of the maze he had created, he reached the herdlands within a day. He galloped on his hands and hooves at a pace neither humans nor buffalo could match. As he approached, he slowed to a stop: a garrison of King's men was building a fort of stone and mortar alongside new iron gates marking the entrance to his lands.

"Under whose orders do you build here?" Isha asked. One earthquake would demolish the abomination.

The soldiers recognized him and dropped their tools. Several prostrated themselves.

"The King ordered us to protect the herdlands." These were not asura but human soldiers under the geas of the King.

Isha raised his sternum and puffed his chest, aware that Hiranyakshipu, or one of his asura, could be watching through their eyes. He looked down his snout and held his gaze. Something about the way the man had spoken unnerved Isha, but he had to let it go.

Isha entered through the new gate. Two bullocks abreast could pass under and through the gate, but Isha had to bow his head. Hiranyakshipu was reminding him to whom he had promised fealty.

## A Lion's Head

He crossed the grassy expanse between the gate and what was a nomadic city of tents built around his home. The sight of grazing buffalo gave him pause. They bellowed their welcome. There were more people than he remembered. Many faces were not of the herd.

"Who welcomes me home?" He reached out his arms as the foreigners closest bowed low with respect.

"Isha!" His wife ran from their domed house. Her hair was coifed. Jangling beads hung from her emerald-green embroidered robes. "He let you come home!"

He breathed in the scent of home and of his love. He had longed for her. She would be no stranger to his passion.

"I must speak to you in private," Chala whispered as they embraced. "How I've missed you, my Isha."

He held her curvaceous frame. She was unchanged, but court life had changed him. He had grown taller in their time apart. His muscles had bulked—had his size grown with the herd or from his proximity to the immortals?

Festivities unfolded around them to welcome him. He was ushered to a pavilion. Drummers and dancers performed to celebrate his return. A storyteller sang the epic of their history, their people's beginning, the summoning of their deities, the mortal world's fall, and their journey to the immortal realm. Another took up the drums to tell their story since the passage to the immortal realm. Feasting, dancing, and merriment took his mind off his concerns.

He was home.

The children—the herd was brimming with children rescued or adopted from other colonies.

He tapped a hoof to the beat. Two dancers representing himself and Chala danced in the centre of a complex movement. The one dressed in dark leather spread his arms and spun hoops in changing geometric patterns. At times, he would spin the hoops from his limbs, neck, and waist. Meanwhile, the one dressed in brightly coloured leathers twirled and leaped. She showered the spectators with colourful feathers and petals as she danced. Guided by the changing tempo of the drums, they danced a spiralling path until the two joined together in unison.

The celebration was not interrupted by the garrison men who joined to watch. Perhaps the King's geas could be broken, and the men could be persuaded to join the herd.

Isha closed his eyes. He was replenished, his energies supercharged, while sitting within the large, healthy population. A weight lifted from his shoulders. The yoke of the First Minister, Lord of the Animals. What did titles mean when he was with the herd? He felt a thousand ethereal tethers between him and his beautiful Chala.

Isha had not forgotten that his powers stemmed from his human herd. Hiranyakshipu could never fathom the type of power that came from his connection to his humans. With no such dependence, the King held no value for mortal lives.

Each time he opened his mouth to ask about the population, he found himself distracted by food and questions: What was it like in the capital? Where was it unsafe to travel? How had the war affected the King? Was he aware of the rebellion?

Isha enjoyed the dancing and drumming. His people were dressed in colourful patterns and ribbons. To his eyes, the vibrancy of colours reflected their success. No longer barefoot, they wore soft, leather-soled shoes.

"Lord Isha, the lands require your blessing. We have four crops on rotation. Third harvest season begins," said one of the shamans.

Isha's rose and swept his gaze over the gathering of his people. Chala appeared at his side, unbidden. She carried a grass-woven tray bearing samples of earth from the four corners of their lands. He held his hands over each and gave his blessing. The earth-bearing tray was ceremoniously passed from person to person until it returned to him again. He cast the tray up, and it flew into the wind, the earth forming a dust devil, dispersing to the four corners of the lands.

The spell marked the end of the party.

As a gift, he cast fireworks to brighten the black sky. The starry night sky of the mortal realm's winter solstice appeared for a fleeting moment as he and Chala danced. By dawn, everyone had dispersed.

# 4

Hiranyakshipu's control over Isha felt like a tick sucking blood from behind his ear. He scratched, wishing to be free of its persistence.

Chala appeared before Isha, beckoning him to follow. Instead, he took her hand and led her into their home. Hiranyakshipu's influence, the seeds of fear, took root. *Will she leave me? Do our people still respect me? What have I done for them but brought them shame and dishonour?*

Chala squeezed his hand, indicating she was aware of his fears. They were one.

He'd been so busy, he hadn't been able to oversee everything and be all he should be. The way Chala's gaze followed the garrison, and the twitch in her ears spoke volumes of her discomfort with them. Maybe the garrison wasn't all bad. Might they be useful for manipulating what the King saw?

Isha and Chala descended deep below ground into their cavernous quarters, used for ceremonies and training shamanic priests. Granite columns warded with spells protected them from observation and eavesdropping. It was the one room Isha could not see when scrying from the capital.

The moss-covered walls induced serenity. The space responded to shamanic magic. With a sweeping motion, he cleaned the area of unfinished works and cobwebs of magic left gathering in his absence. He grounded this energy while renewing the spells fixed to the columns. A ring of soft white sand marked where the ring containing Reesho's ashes lay in the cavern beneath.

"Thank you for clearing the energy." Chala smiled, her face enveloped in exhaustion. "We two have complementary strengths." She held his hands and met his gaze. "I have missed you, Isha."

"I have missed you, Chala." He relaxed. "We have never left so much unspoken between us."

"We have never had anyone or any distance come between us. You did not station those men here—what is the tyrant's scheme?" she asked. "I wouldn't put it past him to have planted spies."

"Chala, I asked for protection. I admit the wall and the garrison caught me off guard. I negotiated for my herd to be kept safe from war," he said. *I am the spy you fear.*

"Our herd," she corrected. "Now, I understand: we are being 'kept safe.' His men make lists. Everyone who enters and leaves. These are our lands. We are not domesticated cattle."

*Even here, we are not safe together?*

"You are safe. Who are these extra people, Chala?"

"Refugees."

"We are all refugees," he said.

"They are recent refugees from lands the King has claimed. Their homes are gone. They have nowhere to go. They have nothing."

"Increasing our numbers is good for the herd," he said. "Has the guard stopped or detained any of them?"

"No, but you're not listening: your king is doing terrible things."

"What concerns me is that he is not doing terrible things here." Isha interrupted her look of admonition with a kiss. "He is unpredictable. My time with him means you are safe."

*I know he does terrible things, my love.*

"We would be safer with you here, Isha."

"Chala, I have not seen you in an age. I've missed you, my love." He stroked her ears. She capitulated. Long after, as she lay in his arms, his gaze was drawn to her mossy green wall. The words in the moss had changed:

*Perseverance guards against loss.*
*Have faith; the path will appear.*
*Look to the verdant moss.*
*The day has come; it is near.*

Chala was stubborn. Isha had to side with the King. Her protective and empathetic nature caused her to sympathize with the refugees, but his pragmatism focused on keeping them safe from the storm. He wondered how much he could tell her. That the King's armies could overrun and enslave them with one command? They were safe as long as the King needed both him and the provisions his people provided.

He could not ask if she was planning to leave him.

Isha spent the morning crossing the herdlands and being seen by the populace. Their crops were prosperous. On request, he created wells, tanks, and caverns. Some had already dug trenches in anticipation, and he revelled at their ingenuity. His pride in his wife overflowed when he heard her leadership praised. They had done well for a bit of independence from him.

## A Lion's Head

By afternoon, Isha began to tire. He felt a gnawing at his navel. What was the feeling of discomfort? Why was he torn between here and there? He caught himself wondering about the latest intrigue—in the aftermath of Holika's death, what would happen to Prahlada?

When Isha asked his warriors if they would go on a hunt, he was startled by their answer: the lands set aside for hunting were being cultivated to feed the growing demand for grain. It was not like Chala to choose farming over hunting. What of the population of bears, wolves, rabbits, and hoofed ones in need of being kept in check through regular culling? What of the meat required for sustenance and trade? He could get no clear answer.

Evening fell before Isha finished his last session with his shamans. They were progressing well under the tutelage of elder shaman Arcuro, despite Isha's prolonged absence.

"Did our warriors tell you of my first encounter with the Asura King?"

"They did, My Lord Isha." Arcuro said. He wore colourful ribbons woven into his clothing. Isha delighted in the effect. The ribbons flew when he twirled, making him look like a bird. Isha had always imagined Arcuro had been a falcon in a past life. As a young child, his attention to detail had helped hone his instincts. Arcuro was a prophet to their people—able to read the future based on his systematic review of events.

"Why leave out the story from our chronicles?" Isha asked, marking Arcuro's discomfort in his dropped gaze.

"Sir, that event is recent," the shaman said.

"It seems to have been forgotten," Isha said.

"Isha, we do not forget you," Chala swept into the room, rescuing the elder who busied himself answering another's questions on mixing herbs.

Was it Isha's imagination, or were all of the shamans suddenly avoiding him? The men and women gathered their belongs, using Chala's entrance as a dismissal.

"Do you find recent events unimportant?" Isha asked Chala. Was he unimportant?

She waited patiently for the men and women to leave. "What has gotten into you, Isha?" she asked.

No, she was here because it was her turn to spend time with him. They were one. He had missed her so much.

They sat close to each other on cushions in the ring of soft sand. False starlight illuminated the room, reflecting the constellations as seen in the mortal realm. He thought about their home, could almost smell it: the fresh grass pastures, the floral bouquets floating on the breeze, the rain. He snapped his fingers, and the floor turned moss green with yellow daffodils sprouting from long-forgotten bulbs underfoot.

"Isha—you remembered!" Once upon a time, they had been the flowers he'd gathered to profess his love for her.

"Yes, my love." He nuzzled her neck as she sighed. They shared a long, quiet rest. He was tired of being away. She was his home.

"I must speak with you, Isha. Please, hear me out," she said. The mirage of moss and flowers disappeared, replaced by the polished, rose-coloured stone floor and white circle of sand.

"I am listening," he said.

"Will you give up your position to stay here with us? You've made your agreements with the King. Maybe now, you could remain here with me?" She looked into his eyes with a desperation born of love.

He wanted nothing more than to say yes. His voice caught in his throat. He closed his eyes as fear clouded his vision. He could not say to her, "we are in too deep."

The God King would be enraged. An army of millions, led by the lowest demon scum, would be camped at the canyon entrance.

Isha shook his head.

She sat before him. She was beautiful. She was home. For the second time, he tried to speak, but his voice caught in his throat. He could not say, "show me the path to freedom."

His people would be arrested on the roads. They would be enslaved, separated, and sentenced to death. Channa the elder would lay dead at his feet while Channa the younger with glazed eyes would lead his troops against the Greater Gods.

*No, no, no.*

Isha rose and strode away from Chala. He looked back at her. She sat there, beautiful and serene. She held out her hands. He took them. He tried to speak for a third time, but his voice caught in his throat again. He could not say, "it's my fault for wanting more than what you and our people give me."

## A Lion's Head

He would be hailed as a hero by the asura, his comrades, and peers, the lords of the capital. He belonged with them. There, he was respected and valued. His work held weight. He stood by the God King's side, victorious. They would win the war.

He shook his head as if it were covered in flies. His eyes met Chala's gaze with equal desperation. The ties that bound them had weakened.

She couldn't save him. Hope evaporated.

"We respect and value you, Isha." She was one with him, for a moment. If only he could trust the future shining in her radiant eyes. She knew nothing of the world outside their borders.

"How will I know of impending danger if I leave his side? His armies will rampage our lands. Our people will be enslaved on the roads. I hold a position of power and trust. I work for our gain," he replied.

"Isha, what if we find another way to go home?" Her ears danced along with her excitement. "What if you did not need to play politics with the King?"

Did she believe the Greater Gods had a plan?

He was one with the King.

"The Greater Gods do nothing for us, Chala. We are too small to be of concern to them. I will find us a way home." Isha wrinkled his nose.

Chala smelled of fear. He had never known her to fear. "I will find it, my love. Don't you see, Chala? My herd will be free to roam. Everything will be all right, my love. I am the lord of the animals."

"Lord of the animals? We don't need to be at the top of the pecking order, Isha. *Our* herds roam free. How are you, lord of the animals? What about the humans?" Chala's voice quivered. "Titles are nothing. There is room for all to live in harmony. We need you here, Isha. I tire of being everywhere all at once." She fought hard against the growing divide between them—to be one with him, to understand him, and to see him. She was tired and resentful. Isha felt her anger and frustration with him. In that shared moment, he felt . . . shame.

A keening pitch drew his attention inwards breaking his connection with Chala. He shook his head in an attempt to free himself from the sound. How was the watcher able to find him from so far away and in this protected sanctuary?

## A Lion's Head

"In these troubling times, we must adapt and assimilate to show our strength." Isha regretted his words. "I approve of your taking in and protecting the refugees. This shows our might. We are great and populous."

"See? We are on the same page," he said. "Would it help for me to send the displaced here?"

"Isha, are you blind?" Her words stung. She stared at him in shock. Her eyes said he had gone too far. "You speak of being the protector of animals and humans. You speak of protecting our herd. Yet you condone the enslavement and war displacing these people?"

"Is the rumour true?" he asked, turning the table on her. His hands held her by the shoulders. She did not look away.

"What rumour?" she replied.

His grip tightened. "Do our people plan to leave here?" he asked. He was one with the king.

She stiffened. His heart sank.

*How had Hiranyakshipu known?*

"What did you hear?" she asked. "What does *he* know?"

*That you will leave me.*

Isha dared not say the words out loud. He could not bear for her to hear his deepest fear.

"Fewer have been venturing out by caravan. When they do, they are single men or elders who should be here, teaching the children," he said.

"Travel is not safe," she replied. "Only those who know their way back are allowed to travel the caravan routes."

"Our warriors are no better than hunters," he said.

"They grow in their skills."

*"They will not leave without the men," the King had said. "Isha, you are like my brother, who I lost. There is nothing I do not share with you. I need you by my side. I want what's best for your people. Bring the men with you when you come back. They can train with my guard and become strong while serving at the palace. In one year, I will give you warriors powerful enough to stand down the strongest asura."*

"I will teach our warriors to be stronger," he heard himself say. "I will take them with me to the palace when I go. They will grow stronger, as I have. We will return once we find the stargates and take you home." In one year he would prove his worth to his herd.

"Our warriors are already trained, Isha. They protect us."

"The King's guards are here for your protection. These lands are impenetrable. You are protected. Our warriors will become more skilled," he countered.

"This is madness, Isha." Chala's voice held a dangerous timbre. "I forbid you to decimate the herd. We have lost enough. Our warriors stand between us and the tyrant's men. To spread us so thin will be the end of us."

"They will return stronger." Maha Isha Sura stood up to his full height, as he had never done before his wife. His frame and horns grew. "I will respect the warriors' right to choose." He glared at her. He was one with the king.

For the first time in their relationship, she shrank back.

His annoyance flared. When did she become weak? The Water Buffalo Herd was strong and held its ground.

Her fear drew his ire.

"I am doing this for our benefit. You want to go home? This is how we will go home."

"No, Isha, not like this. You cannot, please. He has made you his puppet."

"The King wants unity. He wants everyone to benefit from the same freedoms." Isha was not in control of his words. He needed her truths to take hold and give him the strength for what he had to do next.

"To him, humans are expendable," she said.

"In exchange for my service, he safeguards my herd. They are what matters. Let the world burn. My herd—our herd—is safe." Isha was losing his temper. He had never lost his temper with Chala before.

*Let me go. I have lost, Chala.*

"Isha, can you assure me they will come home safely?" She fell to her knees and keened as he stormed from the chamber.

She was right; he was the God King's puppet. She was not safe with him. Not while the King was in control.

The King's control was not complete. The King was ignorant of their ways. "Able-bodied men" excluded women, carters, farmers, and craftspeople. Most of his people wore multiple roles.

Isha sought out Channa the elder. He found his man seated outside the family's yurt, stuffing a sheep's bladder with meat and herbs.

## A Lion's Head

"I was expecting you, My Lord," Channa said as he handed the task to one of his daughters. "Your choices have kept us safe these last few years. We are grateful, My Lord."

"I'm in a bind," Isha admitted.

"I was there when you made your deal with the devil," Channa said. "What does he ask for this time?"

Isha led Channa to one of the caverns used to store farm equipment. He cast a spell to block scrying eyes.

"Lord, what seriousness brings you to me?"

"The King wishes to train our warriors in the capital," Isha said. "How many of our original herd are only warriors?"

"Only warriors? That is tricky. Perhaps a dozen, Lord Isha." Channa replied. "I am a councillor. I am exempt. My son Channa is not."

"He will be in danger."

"He will be an incorruptible man on your side."

"He is not you."

"My son has trained his entire life. Lord Isha, you have always had a member of my family by your side. My ancestors called on you because of need; we serve you out of love," Channa said. Isha had trusted Channa and his ancestors long enough to believe his words were the truth.

"He—any who accompany me—must be given the warrior's choice," Isha asked.

"I will find ask. Those who wish to remain will no longer be called warriors." Channa grinned. "I trust our king invited no women?"

Isha released a sigh. "Able-bodied men—his words, not mine. He holds little value for female asura." His wet eyes recalled Holika's fire dance and demise. Though no more than an acquaintance, she had been kind to him.

Channa patted Isha's shoulder. "I am certain the goddesses take the side of the Greater Gods."

"How I wish they had answered my call," he said.

"They have, Lord Isha, or you would not be here. I believe they have a plan. Will you not choose to remain with us?"

"I cannot." Isha wondered if his faithful Channa knew.


The next day, a large gathering of warriors converged on the training grounds. Those too old or too young, those with families, and those with seasonal contributions were all dismissed.

Chala arrived to watch the process. He saw her nod in approval as she spoke with Channa the elder. It was better this way, another fight would tear them apart.

"I hope you will come to forgive me, my love," he rumbled as she drew near and accepted his embrace.

"You must do as you must." Pointing out the crowd, she said, "The herd loves you and follows where you lead."

Their reconciliation was interrupted by a shouting match. "—My Lord Isha," Davos broke from the heated discussion with his cousin, "please accept me."

"Davos, go back to your wife," Channa the younger said, gripping Davos by the arm to pull him away from their deities. "You bring shame to our family."

Davos prostrated himself on the ground before Isha.

"Go and make children with your intended," Channa the elder chided. "You do not appreciate what you have, Davos."

More boos and catcalls erupted from the growing crowd of spectators.

"I will hear you out, Davos," Isha said, drawing the man away from his audience. He gave Chala a grateful look as she ushered the agitated Channa and his father to continue assessing warriors.

Davos followed him into the privacy of a pavilion. Without his intervention, Davos and his family would be haunted by scandal for years. "Davos, what have you to say?"

"Lord Isha, I. I am a second husband. My wife, she is twice my age. I am nothing more than a stud. How can this be my life?"

"Davos, you will not survive a day where we go," Isha said.

"Lord Isha, let me serve you. I will be your servant," Davos said.

Isha recalled his long-ago wish to send Davos in search of the stargates. He had been distracted by the arrival of Hiranyakshipu that day. He realized he knew little of what had become of Davos since.

"I have no need for servants, Davos. How long have you been married?" he asked

"Four weeks."

"Is she a terrible wife?"

"She—Saida—is a very accomplished woman," Davos replied with a blush.

## A Lion's Head

Isha began to understand the man's reluctance. Saida, a formidable warrior, had married the elder Oumo decades ago. The couple had no children. Perhaps her longing for motherhood had made Davos a victim of the herd's mandate to increase the birth rate. Still, no one had forced Davos into the marriage.

He sized up the petulant man. In another time and place, Davos would have been outcast from the herd. His spirit was not of the water buffalo. He was a lone bull who would not value others until he lost everything. Still, Isha entertained taking the man with him to the capital. His spirit was weak. He would be more susceptible than others to the God King's influence.

"Oumo delivers supplies to the palace kitchens. Let's revisit this request when you accompany him there," Isha said. That should be long enough to cool him down if his request was due to a lovers' spat.

By day's end, Isha stood before Channa the younger and six recruits. To a man, he asked whether they would follow him.

"I will!" the recruits shouted in chorus.

In the days that remained, several people came to Isha and Chala with requests to join the recruits in the capital. One surprise visit was from the younger Channa's mother. She wished to work as a cook in the kitchens to provide the nourishment the recruits would need. Several other elders would join the group to tend to the horses, do laundry, and attend to the recruits' needs.

On the last evening, Chala appeared calm. "You won't be alone, my Isha. I love you. I know I cannot change your mind and have you stay with me," she said as she kissed him. Isha was surprised to receive Chala's blessings.

"The King saw a vision that you and our people would leave me," he blurted out.

Would she leave him?

"I will always be with you, Isha, my love." She placed her hand on his heart. "Come home to me."

It was his turn to cry. She held him until the morning.

There was no alternative. This was the only way for them to survive. He had to keep the God King happy. Where were the Greater Gods? Isha wished they would intervene.

## A Lion's Head

He led the small group from their lands, looking back with regret one last time. Tears flowed from Chala's eyes. Never had he imagined such sadness.

For the sake of the herd, he would keep them all safe.

# 5

When you are dying, your life flashes before your eyes.

What happens when you are born?

Dark matter.

Does the dark exist when there are no senses?

A tree in the cosmos, its canopy reaching high while its roots are buried low. Stardust of an age infinite in space and time. Spiralling, dizzying, tightening, squashing of an errant essence encased within a fixed form. Sensation. The feeling of the sun on closed eyes.

Sinha opened his eyes. He blinked, the world appeared as a golden haze. When his eyes adjusted, it was to focus on a wrinkled old face with dreadlocks gathered in a top knot. His body was draped in an unbleached cotton dhoti with sandalwood beads hung low against his bare navel. Sinha yawned and presented a toothy smile to the infinite cosmic energy, which identified for this moment as an old man.

"He is here," Lord Sakka, Chief of the Greater Gods, said to no one in particular.

## A Lion's Head

They were in a garden ringed with marigolds. A lone baobab tree stood to the side, providing shade under its wide canopy. The ground was covered in grass and flowering plants. The soft sand of the pathway had been swept clean of debris and footprints. The sun drew dappled shadows. Sinha flexed his body as he ran and pounced to catch the flickers of darkness.

"Will he be enough?" The gravel-laden voice—belonging to Ishwara, the energy of creation—took no form. Nevertheless, Sinha peered through the marigolds, hoping to catch a glimpse.

"He is our hope," Surya, the energy of life and the Sun, spoke through sunbeams and sunlight. "He will have an understanding of time. He will not take long to get the job done." Sinha chased Surya's dancing lights until he was tired.

"I have gifted him with knowing intent," Sakka said. "He will see the truth in others to determine what needs to be done."

"He has a seed from the tree of knowledge," said Ishwara, "He will have wisdom to decipher our problem."

"We are pitting fire against fire—what if he becomes our next menace?" Surya asked.

"This is why we temper him. He will have compassion in equal measure."

"Have you each chosen a mortal?" asked Sakka.

"I choose Banchic of Katora Junction." The dry wind swept through the temple grounds, stirring up a whirlwind of dust in response. "He is devout with a long future ahead."

"I choose Oumo of the Water Buffalo Herd," Sakka said, "He is old and wise with a gentle heart."

"Good, for I have chosen his loyal wife, Saida," Surya said. "She is strong and passionate. The conditions have been set."

Sinha played with the shadows. They were not true darkness. He discovered his tail and then his body, which was covered from nose to tail with long, tawny-ginger fur. To his sharp gaze, the world was a dance of colour.

His playful leap ended with a yowl of pain as he landed—that lesson taught him to be cautious. His innocent cry of distress had called the attention of someone else. Someone special. Someone mortal.

———

"Oumo," the woman named Saida called. She wrapped the end of her long, thick, black braid of hair around her wrist.

"I'm looking for an older man. My husband. He answers to the name Oumo," she said to a veiled woman at the haberdashery stand. Accustomed to communicating without knowing the local dialect, Saida mimed a tall, older man.

He had set off with the water gourds. "Where is the well?" She mimicked drinking.

The woman's eyes widened, and she nodded, waving Saida on toward the walled enclosure at the centre of the village. Its spire, marking it a temple to the God Ishwara, rose above the broad canopy of the village's single baobab tree.

Saida and Oumo's caravan train had stopped in Katora Junction to mend broken carts and gear and replenish water. The shrinking oasis existed at the halfway point between the scorched wastelands and desolate rocky highlands circling the capital.

Saida suspected her soft-hearted husband had given the bulk of their supplies to the drought-stricken village. She was no better; she had offered her meagre morning ration of flatbread and pickled vegetables to one of the half-naked children helping with the market stalls. The child had accepted the wrap with a nod of thanks, too hungry to stop and stare at the warrior woman dressed as a man.

The village was waking up. Despite the early hour, a haze of dust hung in the still air, a lingering reminder of the parched landscape. The ground cracked in places forgotten by rain.

Her scalp itched from the heat. She sighed with frustration. Would the gods rescue these people?

Humans were affected by these harsh conditions, not asura. What story had the Asura King told her Lord Isha to manipulate him? No other asura, who were demi-gods when compared to humans, could manipulate the earth. Lord Isha was guilty of creating this inhospitable desert.

Outside the entrance to the temple, Saida slipped off her sandals and placed them beside Oumo's. Stalking her first husband was like hunting deer, so she slowed her pace as she rounded on her quarry. At least she had earned a moment alone with him.

"Oumo?" she called, waving the well-patched headscarf he had left behind in his flight from their wagon. It had been the first article of his clothing that she had bartered for him as his wife.

The lush green grass and foliage of the garden were welcome to eyes accustomed to a wasteland of brown and red. The baobab worked its magic. Saida breathed in the fresh, cool air, and the weight of her regrets lifted. "Oumo?" she called again.

"I'm here," he said. Walking around the tree, she found Oumo seated on a bench hidden from view by the girth of the baobab.

She took a step back, assessing the overlarge beast in his arms. It was the size of a small dog, redder than a cow, but with a serpentine flexibility, allowing it to curl up in Oumo's lap. Its tufted ears were pointed. It's eyes, as strange as a goat's but sideways, stared.

"What is that?" she asked. It was not a dog. She knew dogs, but dogs were all tongue and tail, while this creature was all nose and eyes.

"A cat. He's a big one at that," Oumo said. The cat appeared to be content, curled in Oumo's lap.

Could it read her thoughts? She approached and gingerly sat down on the bench to avoid disturbing it.

"You are upset with me," she began, ignoring the cat. She fixed her gaze on Oumo, whose tears had crusted. She folded the headscarf into a knot, unfolded it, and twisted it into a knot again. Emboldened, she stroked the soft velvet of his cheekbones. The dust fell away.

"Why would I be upset with you? It is I who could not give you the child you want." He did not meet her gaze. "I am old, and you are young. The day I pass, I will be satisfied you are not alone."

"Oumo, don't say that. We have been together for more than a decade," she said, "I care for you."

She did not add, "You are my best friend." Instead, she stared at the verdant grass.

She had married young, and although he was a respected elder, he had not consummated their marriage. She'd mistaken his stoicism and shyness for a lack of desire. After a decade, without issue, their families pressured her to marry again. She wanted to be a mother.

The best-laid plans always fail. She thought it obvious: Davos was the stud, she was the mare. He would never be a replacement for her husband. These last few weeks, the three of them had been confined to a small space. Given Davos's brazen displays of intimacy, she could not blame Oumo for his discomfort.

"He makes you happy as I never could," Oumo said. He hugged the cat. If only he had held her with such affection.

Oumo had it all wrong. She was miserable, but it was all her fault. Her arms fit around his lean waist. He was thinner than usual, gaunt.

"I will not come between you," he said. He kissed the top of her head.

"I will always choose you over him," she said. She kissed Oumo's cheek, tasting the salt of his tears. "I should have adopted one of the orphans. I'm sorry."

It had been a mistake to bring Davos into their lives, but she had to admit she enjoyed bedding him. He was young and handsome, but the infatuation had soon worn off. Davos was arrogant and lazy, and his disrespectful attitude gnawed at her.

Davos had shown his true colours when he'd thrown himself at Lord Isha's feet and begged to join him in the capital. Saida's ego had been in tatters. All she could do was walk away with her head held high. The whispers followed her as the summer wind rustled leaves in the forest. He had brought shame to their union. From that night, she had avoided him. She was not stupid.

Davos was ambitious. Where was he trying to go, and who was he trying to be? Saida would have cast him aside if it were not for Lady Chala. That night, Lady Chala had come to watch Saida at dusk as she worked through a complicated technique with her staff.

"Nice form," Chala had said. "'Busy the mind and the body to bring sleep and ease a troubled mind,'" she quoted.

"Lady Chala!" Saida had bowed her welcome. She adored her goddess. She offered Chala a share of the remaining apples from her dinner basket. "What brings you to me this evening?"

"I am glad you are alone. What I say must not be shared, not even with Oumo. He will make one last delivery of vegetables to the palace. You can remain with the herd *or* go with Oumo. The herd will not be here when you return." Chala waited with patience as Saida took in the information.

"The herd . . . will go home?" Saida whispered. Did she dare to dream? "What of Oumo?"

"He wishes to take one last delivery. He wishes to breathe his last breath in service to Lord Isha."

"He would," Saida said, wrapping her long braid tightly around her wrist.

"He wants you to go with me. You are my warrior—the choice is yours," Chala said.

"How did you find a pathway back?"

Chala smiled and liberated Saida's braid from her fretful hands. Holding Saida's hands, she said, "I did not know how to reach the Greater Gods. Then, one night—frustrated and afraid—I took my bovine form. I whispered to the universe: 'Come and relieve me of the burden I carry. So much is going wrong.' They caught me by surprise when they responded." In that moment, Chala's face softened. Tears brimmed in her eyes.

"What did they say?" Saida asked. She squeezed her Lady's hands tight with reassurance.

"That not everyone can come home." Chala's voice broke; her stoic mask did nothing to hide her deep emotions from her long time student. "What of you? Will you come with us when we go?"

"What of Davos?" Saida asked, trying to buy time. She wanted a child, but what life would a child have without a herd?

Chala's eyes narrowed, and her ears flicked. "Davos will be delivered to Lord Isha with the last delivery of vegetables to the palace. He has sealed his fate. You must decide yours," said Chala.

Davos was being cast out of the herd. He had unleashed a scandal. Already, ugly rumours circulated about how she, an accomplished warrior, could not satisfy two husbands. It was her right as a warrior to release both men from marriage and remain with the herd.

What home did she have if not with Oumo?

"I will remain with Oumo until the end, Lady Chala." She'd spent her life with Oumo—how could she abandon him now?

"Are you sure?" The concern in Chala's voice brought tears to her eyes. Was she making a mistake?

"I am sure. My life is tied to Oumo's. I can have no life without him." Nor would she be able to live with herself for leaving him.

"There is a slight chance you can find your way to us," Chala said. A single tear fell to her lap.

"Wouldn't that be wonderful?" Saida said, wiping her eyes. The two sat in silence for a time, with Lady Chala continuing to hold Saida's hands. Speaking less about plans brought them closer to fruition.

"You are strong," Lady Chala had said. "May the universe protect you in this life and the next. I will miss you, my warrior."

The rustling leaves of the baobab tree drew dancing shadows on the grass and flowers. A cough at the temple's gate caught Saida's attention. There, a boy—no, to her sharp eyes he was a young man dressed to pass as a boy—stood. He was stocky despite his pronounced rib cage. He had no facial hair, and his shoulder-length hair was tied back into a ponytail. He wore little, nothing but a pair of shorts. They were trespassers to his village temple. She could not decide if his furrowed eyebrows were angry or curious as he stared at them. Or was he staring behind them?

Turning her head, she was startled to see a third set of footprints had joined hers and Oumo's, an old stranger in the clothes of a priest walked the temple grounds. Where the man stepped, plants grew, their flowers bleached white. He left behind an ivory carpet—was this one of the Greater Gods?

Oumo gave a start. They both stood to welcome the stranger, who made Oumo look youthful.

"Oumo and Saida of the Water Buffalo Herd," the man said. Nodding toward the young man at the gate, he called, "Banchic of Katora Junction, join us."

The bare-chested boy stood for a long moment, captivated like a startled deer. He checked himself for loose hairs and dusted the sand from his shorts and feet. Approaching, he bowed low to the god.

Oumo stared at the old man, his mouth agape. Saida grabbed his hand and pulled him down, wincing at the creak in his knees. The three prostrated themselves before the old man.

"Be seated," he commanded.

She envied the youth who dropped himself into a cross-legged seat on the soft, cool grass in one fluid motion. The god seated himself on the raised stone bench under the ash tree.

Saida looked around and found a stone for Oumo, who was too stiff to sit on the ground. She helped lower his arthritic body. She, however, would stand. Lady Chala was her

Goddess. Any other god would have to earn her respect.

The cat leaped into Oumo's lap and began purring.

"Is it chance or coincidence bringing the three of you to this garden today?" Up close, the man was as dark-skinned as Banchic. Blue waves crashed in his eyes.

"Who are you, Sir, ah . . . Great Lord?" Banchic asked.

"For today, I am a storyteller," he said.

Saida couldn't help but stare. It was clear to all three of them: he was a god. Maybe he thought hearing the truth would be too much for them. Except for his eyes, the god appeared human, unlike the buffalo-human forms of Lord Isha and Lady Chala. Was he one of the Greater Gods? Saida shivered, cold with anticipation. What would a greater god want with the three of them?

"Great Lord, may I ask, what is that?" Banchic pointed at the creature in Oumo's arms.

"That, my dear boy, is Sinha."

"Surely he's too small to be a lion," Banchic asked, translating sinha to mean lion.

"He's a cat," Saida whispered in accented trade-tongue. She offered a comforting smile.

Banchic bristled as the cat began to take an interest in him.

"Praise to your teacher," the god said. "You are correct. Sinha does not meet the description of a lion. For the time being, he is a cat."

"I've never seen a cat before," Banchic said. The cat let out a meow and wriggled out of Oumo's arms in protest. It leaped to join the god on his bench. A stray silver dreadlock from his topknot diverted the cat's attention. The feline batted it before sniffing the god's fragrant sandalwood garland.

"An easy mistake, Banchic," Oumo said. "I saw one once before, as a child."

"Cats as a species were the canary in the coal mine, a warning we should have heeded. This realm is not for them or for you," the storyteller said. "You see, the immortal realm was made as a trap to contain the asura.

"We built this realm to catch the asura reincarnates of the celestial gatekeepers Jaya and Vijaya. You see, long ago, the four bearers of cosmic knowledge arrived at Ishwara's gates." He swatted away the cat's paws. "Now, imagine the gatekeepers' confusion when the princes appeared as cherubs, naked toddlers."

## A Lion's Head

"They were turned away?" Banchic's horrified look was directed at the cat, though it appeased the god. As the cat started to sniff him, Banchic fidgeted sideways in an attempt to avoid its nose.

Saida bit her hand to keep herself from laughing; better him than her.

"Yes. Never underestimate appearances. This cat is not a cat in the same way those princes were not children."

"The gatekeepers denied them entry, taunting beings as old as the universe." The storyteller's chuckle held his unease. "As you might expect, the princes were not amused. They cursed the two brothers to thrice wander the Samsara, until they overcame greed, anger, and lust." He cocked his head to listen before a rooster's call sounded beyond the temple walls. "Those with great knowledge are often limited in compassion, if you ask me. You don't see any shrines dedicated to them, do you?"

"What happened then?" Saida asked, hoping her curiosity might quicken the pace of the story. She and Oumo had to return to their wagon for the mid-day inspection.

"The gatekeepers' reincarnates hold a grudge because their master, Lord Ishwara, couldn't break the curse," the storyteller said.

"Why hold a grudge against the one trying to save you?" Banchic covered his mouth with his hands.

"Tell me, young man: why else would they seek to destroy all of creation?" the god asked sternly.

"Isn't it karma that a servant should turn on his master in the next life?" Banchic swallowed hard and dared to meet the god's gaze.

"The brothers accrued great karma in their service to Ishwara," the storyteller said, "Vijaya was reborn as Hiranyaksha—I am sure all three of you know what he did."

"He destroyed our lands," Oumo had been quiet up until then. The cat returned to his lap and resumed its purr.

"You see, Hiranyaksha held the earth goddess Bhumi hostage under the cosmic seas. We—Varaha, the boar-headed warrior, sent him into the next life while saving Bhumi. To this day, he holds her tectonic plates stable." Lord Sakka winked at Saida.

Saida closed her eyes and sighed.

Banchic groaned.

"Hear now, sir," Oumo said. "what are you suggesting?"

"The event was earth-shattering. Land masses crashed into each other, and some sank while the Himalayas rose from the sea. We—the Gods tried to save your people from extinction," the storyteller reached a crescendo.

"Why bring our people here?" Oumo asked.

"Humans cannot live in the heavens or the hells. This realm is neither heaven nor hell as long as humans live here," he replied.

"Lord, why are you telling us this?" Oumo asked.

"The time to return has come." Lord Sakka met their astonished gazes. The waves of the cosmic seas crashed in his sapphire eyes.

"But what of the Asura King? Is he not trapped here, as are we?" Banchic asked. "How can we return while he reigns? His armies took my father and brothers. I will be next. Our people are dying."

"The boy speaks the truth," Oumo said.

The old man looked from Banchic to Oumo as if weighing their souls. Oumo had once told Saida, "We mortals should never question the gods or gain special notice."

The god pointed an index finger and opened his mouth as if to answer, but was interrupted by the sound of the villagers outside the temple walls—the raucous scraping, pounding, and screeching as they worked wood and metal. He continued down his original vein. "The gatekeeper Jaya was reborn as your Asura King," he said.

"You jest," said Banchic.

"His son, the prince regent, was the only being standing in his way." The god's stern gaze locked on the cat. "Until now."

# 6

The moss wall was all that remained of her.

Chala had left him. Vanished without a trace when the sun crossed the morning horizon. The tethers holding him to the herd were gone. Where he had once felt thousands, he now felt a few dozen. All who remained accompanied him, a scattering of elders and a few remaining herdsmen. He could feel several on distant trade routes. He felt as though a thundering hedonic waterfall had been blocked with only a few drops of water left to escape. The sudden dearth of power had caused him to lose consciousness. Lucky for him, he had been in his quarters at the time.

Weak as a mortal, Channa had helped him to his feet. "The people are gone, My Lord, but I am here with you," he said.

Had Channa practiced this moment, knowing Chala's intent? Had Isha been kept in the dark on purpose? Rage burned his mind while despair corroded his heart. Depression set in as his regrets buzzed around his head like flies.

"You knew," Isha said.

"I was forewarned, My Lord. I'm sorry. Lady Chala presented me with a warrior's choice. She shared no details of where or how they went, only that they would go."

"You did not ask?"

"My loyalties are with you and the herd, My Lord. To ask would be to put the herd at risk," Channa said.

"You speak in riddles!" Isha bellowed, though he knew the truth of Channa's words.

"I speak from my father's council, My Lord."

"Where *is* your father?" Isha's words were punctuated with anger. Dependent on the older Channa's counsel, he felt twice betrayed.

"He will serve our Lady Chala as I serve you." Though Channa's wide eyes and dry lips betrayed his fear, his act of courage enveloped Isha in a wave of admiration and gratitude. Isha heard the ghost of Channa's ancestor whisper, "I will protect you."

His anger faded. Maha Isha Sura would not fall to his knees like a spurned lover bawling for his Chala. He would not. Instead, he breathed deeply to calm the madness of emotion stirring within. How much did the King know?

He did not ask the King for permission to leave. As soon as the night demons had dissipated, he galloped to the herdlands. She had left an inscription on the moss wall, knowing he would see it:

*My beloved, Isha Sura,*
*I take our people home.*
*You will find me where the moss is green.*
*Ptehíŋchala Ska Wiŋ of the Water Buffalo.*

Isha touched the mark that read "Chala."

He touched the wall with his magic. Did the moss hold the secret of his lady's whereabouts? No trace. At least none were revealed to his sorcery. His powers were limited. His wife and his herd vanishing had caught him unaware. They were not dead. Death left a trace. The harvest was gone. The herdlands were vacant. He could not fathom how Chala had removed people and food from under the watch of the King's garrison.

Where had they gone? The people had been here three days prior. No one remained. Even the garrison was gone with no signs of violence. He could only assume that wherever they were, they were safe.

Isha needed time to think. He tried not to think past the day, let alone the week. How could he exist without Chala? He had to find her. She and he were one no more.

The void, the lack, brought him to his knees. "Chala, where are you? I need you." He prayed to the wall. "I am nothing without you."

Alone, tears fell free from his eyes. He had nothing of hers left except the moss-covered wall. He fell to his knees and wept until he was as empty as his lands.

What would Hiranyakshipu make of the disappearance of his herd?

*He will ridicule me.*

More important, there was nothing left to provision the God King's army. Those who remained would not be safe. Isha needed his people. They needed him.

*I will round them up. I will protect them.*

Isha read the writing on the wall again.

*I will find you, Chala.*

His herd was safe. They had to be safe.

He would find them.

# 7

The storyteller god had dismissed the mortals. A gentle rustle of leaves overhead provided a soothing accompaniment to Banchic's rhythmic sweeping. Saida drew water from a small well and poured it into the gourds Oumo had brought.

"This is where you come in," Sakka said, addressing Sinha.

*Me?* Sinha's mind voice could only be heard by those who knew how to listen. Out of the corner of his eye, he spied Oumo's head turn to stare in surprise. Could the older mortal hear him?

*I am a cat.* Sinha had his teeth in Sakka's loose grey dreadlock following a solid urge to dislodge a star, planet, or at least some stardust contained within.

"You are no more a cat than I am a storyteller, Sinha." Sakka pulled his hair out of Sinha's mouth and stood, dropping him to the ground.

*This is a magnificent body.* His agile form twisted mid-air and landed on four feet.

Sakka paced the yard so they were out of hearing. "We put you in the body of a cat for a reason. You will have only one chance to catch Hiranyakshipu by surprise." He fixed Sinha with a stern look.

*I'm to defeat the Asura King?* Sinha returned his look. *As a cat?*

"Yes. You will know when the time comes to transform to your true form." Sakka said.

*Why must I defeat him? He has done no harm to me,* Sinha thought.

"His anger cannot be extinguished. He will not stop until he has consumed all of existence." Sakka paced.

*Does that justify a kill?* Their conversation was interrupted by Saida's exclamation while Oumo—preoccupied with listening for Sinha's mind voice—had let precious water spill out of the gourd he held. Did Sakka know Oumo could hear him?

"All of creation is threatened while he lives. He is invincible to all but you," Sakka replied.

*Is there no other way?* Sinha asked.

"It is this, or plunge all of the realms of existence into another Armageddon. Mankind will not survive," Sakka said, "More will die than be reborn. There won't be enough to repopulate."

Sinha puffed himself up. *There are other beings occupying the mortal realm. Why depend on humans?*

"Humans are necessary for balance; they are central to Samsara," he said simply. "The mortal realm anchors the higher and lower realms. Without its stability, chaos reigns."

*What of me?* Sinha asked. *Where do I fit?*

Sakka let out a long breath, gazing at the marigolds. The sunlight and shadow falling through the canopy of the ash tree provided a warm and comforting space. Banchic's sweeping and the noise from outside the temple grounds reminded them they were not alone. Saida finished filling the gourds and conversed with Banchic as he swept. Oumo sat, feigning meditation.

"You are unique, Sinha. A hybrid," Sakka answered. "You are an animal, man, and asura. There is no being like you. You were not born. We *three* willed you into being."

*To kill an invincible asura?*

"The King's invincibility is locked in this riddle:

> Death cannot be experienced by him
> while the sun or moon crosses the sky,
> when he is inside or outside a dwelling,
> while in the air or touching earth,
> in the heavens or in the hells.
> Any weapon, palm, or fist cannot kill him,
> borne by human, deity, demon, or animal."

*And, if I fail?* the cat asked.

Sakka sat low to the ground on his haunches. His gaze met the cat's eyes with a grim look of determination. "You won't."

He dematerialized in a frangipani-scented breeze.

Sinha sat surrounded by ivory flowers and the sunlight dancing with the shadows.

The three mortals remained in the garden—*why had Lord Sakka introduced him to these three?*

Ears pricked forward, tail twitching, Sinha watched Banchic cross the threshold. His bare feet made faint impressions on the dusty earth. Each sweep sent clouds of dust swirling into the air. The excursion brought a thin sheen of sweat to his brown skin.

Captivated by the rhythmic sway of the broom, Sinha's hips shook in anticipation. His body responded before his mind could, and he pounced on the broom as it came into range.

"Hey! Stop that," exclaimed Banchic, dropping the broom in surprise.

Sinha's interest evaporated. His nose twitched, and he sneezed. Not liking the dust on the ground, he decided to climb the tree.

"The Great Lord has left, has he? I don't have enough time. The temple is supposed to look abandoned," Banchic said.

"Banchic, let us help," Saida said. "If we had known, we would not have stepped so callously. Is it because it is Ishwara's temple?"

"Yes, the Asura King banned worship. But we have an agreement with the guards: make the temple look abandoned and bribe them. The problem is, we can't afford the bribe," said Banchic.

"I have heard said, when Ishwara's well runs dry, a hero will be nearby—this is that well?" Oumo said.

"There's barely any water in it," Saida said.

"Maybe it is time this well went dry. I believe the storyteller god was introducing us to our hero here," Oumo said.

"You're saying Sinha is the hero who will defeat the Asura King?" Saida asked.

"We are not warriors. Can you imagine *us* storming the capital and breaking down the palace gates to get a cat inside?" Banchic doubled over with laughter. "Perhaps he can accompany me when they conscript me." He turned to see Saida's serious look, composed himself, wiped tears from his eyes, and added, "No disrespect intended, ma'am."

"Banchic, we're headed to the palace," Saida said

Banchic gasped. "You are herdspeople."

"That is correct." Oumo glanced at Sinha, watching from his perch in the baobab. "Sinha, sir, will you find us before we leave?"

*I will find you, Elder.* Sinha replied with an audible meow.

"Oumo, you think the cat—" Saida said.

"—Finish your work here, Banchic. Give your goodbyes, and be at the temple gates when we ride past." Oumo took Saida's hand and the water gourds and hurried from the yard.

Sinha understood Oumo and Saida's role. But why had the gods chosen this young man?

Banchic pulled water from the tiny well using a bucket and wheel pulley system. Sinha jumped to the rim to investigate. The rope was short. The well was not deep. He knocked the first bucket Banchic drew back in and heard a satisfactory splash as it hit the water.

"Please don't do that! I need to get clean." Banchic pulled a second bucket of water out of the well, keeping it away from the cat. The bucket was only a quarter-way full. He used scant water to wash the sweat and dust from his hands, body, and face. His body dried in the heat. "Used to be you could pull up a full bucket. I've never seen it. My mother said the water once had the power to heal."

Sinha sniffed the bucket. The water was nothing special. He followed Banchic into the temple, sneezing upon encountering the heavy sandalwood incense.

Banchic murmured a prayer in the shrine room and placed a semicircle of white flowers before the single oil lamp. The walls were adorned with wooden panels painted with scenes of gods and goddesses engaged in celestial dances. Sitting cross-legged on the cold stone floor, his palms touching, he thanked Ishwara. He bowed thrice before standing to pull a rope hanging from the wall.

A great bell rang, its loud and clear notes reverberating back to silence.

Sinha jumped. He fixed his four legs out, and his fur stood on end. His instinct was to protect Banchic, but he did not know from what. He could do nothing as a cat. Banchic picked him up and hugged him.

"Hey, that's the morning bell—better late than never." Banchic carried Sinha out of the temple. He stepped around the grassy border of the yard, leaving the sand pathway undisturbed.

They walked out into a street bracketed by derelict homes. Some were carved into the limestone of the canyon. "There used to be more of us. Last year, the village relocated into the caves; if the guards don't see healthy adult men, they can't take them."

People were unpacking and organizing stalls along the main road. Most wore simple garb; unbleached homespun wraps or robes and head coverings.

"We make ourselves useful. Otherwise, we'll end up rounded up and vanishing like the people in the more remote tribes. The guards on the caravan trains are nicer than those who go to war."

"Banchic, who are you talking to? What are you carrying?" A small, stern woman stood in their path with her hands on her hips. Her clothing covered her from head to toe, exposing only her eyes. "The bell was late!"

"We had a divine visitor at the temple, Mother. See? The temple flowers have turned white." Banchic offered her the one tucked behind his ear.

"You have got to get back to the caves. I will not have you taken by the guards," she said.

Sinha could read her intention to safeguard her son. Banchic was his mother's world.

"The divinity left this cat at the temple. I'm taking him to Mani."

"You will find him there." She pointed at a closed tent. "I don't know what he's thinking, setting up a prayer tent in the middle of a market. Daft fool believes there will be faithful, seeking a blessing. Banchic, there are more captives. Poor souls—may they find freedom in this life."

"And in the next," Banchic replied. "Mother, I met herdspeople."

"They have offered you safe passage?"

Sinha stared into the woman's face in disbelief. Her words suggested hope, but her heart was breaking. Banchic was oblivious to his mother's pain.

"I will join the rebellion," he said.

"If you must." Her words fell flat. She stared long into his face. "Go, then!" she said and returned to her work, unpacking haberdashery items for her stall.

Banchic paused to gaze back at his mother, a wistful smile on his lips. Sinha understood. Were the situation different, he would have no reason to leave. The mother's intent to keep her son safe meant pushing him away.

Banchic crushed Sinha's body tighter against his body, a physical reassurance against a feeling of loss. Humans were complicated.

They were bathed in a deafening wall of sound when the tent flap opened. An elder priest tied the tent flap open, and paused to enjoy the cool morning air. Dressed in the same garb as Sakka, High Priest Mani wore a white dhoti and a garland of fragrant sandalwood beads. He had the holy mark of divinity tattooed on his forehead: a cross, each arm representing one of the four elements, curled around a single dot—the spirit that bound them.

"Banchic! Where did you find a cat?" Mani's bald head was covered in a sheen of perspiration. Behind him was a line of senior priests, chanting and clashing symbols.

"Sir, he was left at the temple." Banchic let go of Sinha and bowed to his teacher. "Also, the temple flowers have turned white. We had a visitor." He told his teacher of his encounter.

"Hmm. Miracle upon miracles. May you live in interesting times, indeed!" his teacher replied. He reached out a tentative hand to the cat.

Sinha sniffed Mani's fingers.

"We are honoured. Welcome to our humble village of Katora," Mani said, bowing his head.

Sinha pressed his head into Mani's open hand. The priest smelled of incense. He sneezed.

"He blesses me." Mani chuckled, wiping his hand on his sleeve. "When Ishwara's well is dry, a hero will be nearby. Banchic, keep an eye on the well today. I suspect the prophecy will come true. " He looked to the heavens. "Lord Ishwara, protect. We are grateful. Keep your new friend close to you, and go with my blessing."


A shrill warning sounded from a villager monitoring the guard's movements. Mani waited to hear the coded series of calls before returning to the tent, calling an end to their prayer.

A trickle of people started to crowd the narrow street. Fine, colourful clothing distinguished them from the locals. Sinha's whiskers twitched with curiosity. Banchic carried him back to the temple. He leaped to a better vantage point on the wall overlooking the flurry of activity unfolding on the bustling street below. Carts rattled by. Vendors haggled over prices. His ears were assaulted by the rhythmic clang of metal on metal as workers repaired wagons. The stands sold handcrafted sandstone ornaments, medicinal herbal tonics, and cooked food. A covered platform staged a minstrel, who played his three-stringed setar as a soundtrack to the shouts, bellows, and hums. An audience of guardsmen in blue and merchants in colourful garb gathered to eat and drink.

Sinha recognized Mani, dressed in the robes of a village elder, his tattooed forehead wrapped in a headscarf as he manned a stall serving water in clay cups. Children who were too young to be noticed by the guardsmen carried them to a small group.

Sinha darted through the crowd, his curiosity and the need to know driving his steps. In what would pass for a village square was a group of men individually bound at the wrist. They were also tied to each other with long ropes, forcing them into four single-file lines. Their feet were cracked and bleeding. Several cried while others prayed. Some, too despondent or beaten, hung their heads. The captives' once vibrant clothing was covered with dust and sand.

Even their guards knew they had done nothing to deserve this. Sinha stretched tense muscles. But how could he put a stop to it?

"Stop! You can't!" Banchic's shrill voice cracked with distress.

Sinha's hackles rose. Without thinking, he ran along the top of the temple wall in the direction of Banchic's voice. Banchic stood before the well. The hot midday sun beat down without mercy, casting long, harsh shadows across the dusty ground. The imposing silhouettes of five guards shadowed Banchic's lean frame.

Sinha leaped down and bounded to the yard. Five men in dark blue uniforms stood there, cudgels hanging from their waists. Their leader, a stern-faced man with a weathered face and arms like tree trunks, brandished a shovel, his eyes fixed on the well.

Undeterred by the guards, Banchic stood his ground, his unwavering voice ringing out. "You can't fill the well! Every drop of water is precious!"

"Stand aside, boy. The will of His Supreme Holiness must be obeyed." The man's voice was rough with authority. His brow furrowed in consternation as his grip tightened on the shovel handle. "Move aside."

"I won't," Banchic said. The older man sighed. Banchic's feet dug deep furrows in the sand as two guardsmen dragged him from the well.

How dare they lay hands on Banchic!

Sinha leapt at the leader with a yowl, fur on end, claws ready.

The seasoned guard caught him in mid-air. Time slowed to a crawl as the men took in the situation and erupted in laughter.

Sinha spat and hissed. His claws swatted the air but failed to reach his foe. His energies were soon spent. He had no words. He had no strength with which to defeat the men. He was a cat. With great resignation and fatigue, he let his body go limp.

"Never knew a temple to be guarded by a cat," said the leader. Sinha grimaced as he was sized up. The man whistled. "He's a beauty."

As if by magic, the tension of the situation evaporated.

"Please, sir, don't hurt him." Banchic broke loose from his captors and fell on his knees, begging.

"Boy, we won't harm him. In return, how about you stay out of harm's way? This isn't the village's only well. Your people will not die of thirst." The guard's eyes had softened.

Sinha realized the guard was following orders. He intended to keep his family fed.

Banchic carried a dumbfounded Sinha to the bench under the baobab tree, where they watched as the guards converged on the well. The men had brought wheelbarrows containing large stones, sand, and dirt. Sinha sniffed the boy's arms and face. He was unharmed. His sharp nose picked up the smell of lotus flowers.

"Sinha," Banchic's voice was quiet, deep, gravel-like, "it's only rocks." Banchic glanced at the well before returning his attention to Sinha. The guards poured sand over the rocks, leaving enough space for a concrete solution to harden and cure in the sun. "It could be worse. They wouldn't dare use excrement. Not that it would matter."

"Do you feel their intentions, Sinha? Not so simple, eh? They are full of fear and doubt. They worry they bring my wrath upon themselves."

Sinha sat at attention. This was not Banchic. Lord Ishwara controlled the boy's body. He sat up and touched nose to nose in respect.

"Yes," the god-possessed Banchic continued. "It is not their intention to desecrate the well, Sinha. There is more than meets the eye."

*But they are sealing your well!* Sinha jumped to the ground and arched his back with a hiss.

"Correction: they have sealed *a* well. There will come a time for your righteous anger. I forbid you to harm humans. Their lives are too short without our meddling. One asura seeking dominion over all beings is enough. Do not become another Asura King. You have one mission. One chance. Distraction is not an option."

*How will I defeat the Asura King if I am too weak to fight a man?* Sinha asked. He padded after Ishwara-Banchic into the cool interior of the stone temple. They climbed the steps to the shrine room. Wooden panels covered three of the walls.

The god stopped before a tall panel depicting Hiranyaksha's death. On it, a boar-headed man stood before a fanged demon holding a round-bellied mother goddess under spirals and stars.

"One is often enough. One can be stronger than a dozen, Sinha." Ishwara ran a finger along the outline of the demon. "See this asura? He was so angry he set the continents adrift. Mortals died in the great flood, but many who refused our help survived. Amazing!" Ishwara tapped the carving and smiled when the wooden panel returned a hollow sound. "I voted against the majority: I was against creating you. I disagree with the idea of fighting fire with fire. I had hoped we could ask Hiranyakshipu what he wanted. Sadly, my brethren lack diplomacy. Too often, we gods fail to hear the needs of our followers. How can I expect them to listen to the demands of their enemy?" He snapped youthful fingers, and the panel swung open as if on hinges. Sinha accompanied Ishwara inside.

The only light came from the flickering lamps in the shrine room. The niche was enough to hold one person. It contained a small stone basin, two hands wide. Sinha chirped with curiosity. He walked over and tried to tip over the bowl but it was fixed to the ground and full of water. He dipped a curious paw and felt the energy transmit from his paw to the rest of his body. His tail stood up. He was invigorated.

"You feel it, yes? The water has the power to heal," Ishwara said. "The first wave of refugees used these waters to adapt to their new life here. Many were injured when they fled the mortal realm. You see, Sinha, all things of value should be made scarce. When it was no longer needed, the water was lost." Ishwara sat cross-legged, and their gaze locked. "Sinha, no demons or asura travel with today's caravan. You met a couple from the Water Buffalo Herd. The old man will take you to where you need to go."

Ishwara-Banchic closed his eyes. Sinha touched him, nose to nose, and the god's presence evaporated leaving the scent of blooming lotus flowers lingered in the air.

The boy stirred as if from slumber. He rubbed his bleary eyes, stretched his limbs, and took in his surroundings. His bare feet and legs shivered, cold from contact with the stone floor. Banchic blinked several more times. "How did I get here?"

Sinha meowed in response. Banchic could not hear his thoughts.

Banchic's gaze rested on the water basin and the open panel to the shrine room. Rising to his feet, Banchic dipped a curious finger into the water. His eyes widened in surprise. He bowed thrice to the water source. "Oh! Lord Ishwara! Ishwara, King of Gods! You are great! I'm sorry I ever doubted you. I will never doubt you again!"

## A Lion's Head

He looked at Sinha. "Do you think I offended him?" Sinha returned his look.

Banchic closed the panel after making sure he could open it again. "It's a miracle!" He sat with his back to the panel, eyes darting at the shadows. He looked into Sinha's eyes and said, with a wisdom that had been absent a moment before, "Ishwara's well ran dry today. Go, Sinha. Go be the hero this realm needs."

Sinha left Banchic sitting by the secret door. All but two of the guards had taken their wheelbarrows and equipment and left, one stood in the small gateway to keep the curious out, while the other stood watch as the cement dried. "Nothing to see here," the first repeated.

Sinha observed their deepening fears as he walked over the wet cement. Glancing back, he was satisfied with the paw prints he had left behind.

Ishwara had said he was forbidden from harming humans—If the Gods were so powerful, why hadn't they forbidden the King from harming humans?

# 8

When you are dying, your life flashes before your eyes.

His creation in the temple garden. Banchic sweeping. Oumo crooning. Saida's deadly dance with a staff. Rocking to sleep in a burrow of straw. Those had been his happiest days full of life preceding his first meeting with the Prince. His first kill. The targeted animosity and fear of the court asura. His guilt for ever losing his temper, albeit righteous. Sinha had already been feared before the King had set him to ridding the realm of its demons.

"Is this what I was made for?" Sinha roared into the darkness. He had never been so close to death, his body crushed and torn by the aftermath of the fall.

In darkness, his body began to heal. He ached, and he itched. The pain of bones knitting themselves together was excruciating. He had held himself aloft past dusk. How long before he would be strong enough to push through his burial stones and dig his way to the surface? His body was frozen. All he had left were his memories.

The light had been so bright. Smells from the

wagon of herbs, onions, and garlic had made him sneeze. Or was it the dust? A land without rain. The water buffalo had been content to eat the dried grasses stacked high on the wagon roof and brought down by human hands. Wood, used sparingly to cook food, weighed down the dried grass against the foul winds. The nights were cold. The humans had dressed in layers and slept together for warmth. The land was harsh. Nothing could thrive without divine intervention.

---

Sinha remembered Oumo. He had been an oasis. A single recognizable being amid the chaos of the village of Katora. People were everywhere: guards, traders, and villagers—none of whom smelled or felt safe. Oumo was familiar and safe.

Oumo was exiting Mani's prayer tent. He wore a coarse linen shirt, shalwar pants, and a dark grey vest embroidered with a simple curling vine pattern. He protected his anonymity with a hat and scarf as he would against the sun and sand. He carried the drinking gourd of holy water slung over his shoulder, positioned protectively away from the crowd.

*Oumo!* Sinha's excitement carried through his mind voice.

The man stood for a moment, his rheumy eyes adjusting to daylight. Sinha flicked his tail, made a graceful leap. and landed squarely in his path. Startled, Oumo stumbled backward into the tent. Before he could regain his composure, Sinha had wound himself around Oumo's legs in a silent plea for attention.

Oumo chuckled, bent down to scoop up Sinha, and cradled him in strong arms. "Sinha!" Oumo flattened the cat against his body as he walked through the crowd. "Come with me. My wagon is a bit of a walk away."

Several guards and workers had drawn a crowd of spectators as they blocked the street, removing a stiff, broken wheel from its axle. Oumo and Sinha were able to pass without notice.

"I'd wager the Gods had a hand in staging that distraction for us to pass unnoticed." Sinha could hear Oumo's barely audible whisper. "As our friend said, cats are rare. We will be safe when we reach my wagon. If anyone asks, I'll say I bred you in the Herdlands."

Sinha could not control his pleasure at being held by Oumo. His purrs mingled with the sound of the busy road, a rhythmic melody to drown out the chaos of the world around them. Oumo's arms cradled him tighter. The older man dodged foot traffic and skirted handcarts until he reached a large, covered wagon loaded high with dried grasses and firewood. As he walked, his head scarf drifted open, revealing his tanned, wrinkled face.

"Hey, old man," a masculine voice called out, "we sent you for water. You come back with a cat!" Oumo slowed his steps and raised a hand in greeting.

Sinha noted his abrupt caution.

"Davos, I trust you took the buffalo to the troughs?" Oumo shifted Sinha to one arm so he could clasp the arm of the much younger man, his face finely chiselled and sun-weathered. The two men shared the thinning hairline and prominent nose of the herdspeople. Davos could pass for Oumo's son.

"Not a worry, Oumo. Our beautiful Saida has taken them this time," Davos said, his expressive blue eyes hinting at arrogance as he mentioned Saida. His playful smile reflected the lightness of youth.

"And every time," Oumo grumbled under his breath.

As the two men walked, Sinha noticed Davos's left foot pointed inwards, forcing him to walk with a limp. He sensed a buried tension behind the man's bitten lip. Was it arrogance or hatred? Elitism or ambition? The emotions were gone as quickly as they appeared, leaving Sinha with no doubt: Davos knew how to manipulate and take advantage of his fellows.

"I picked him up in the village. He's a big fellow. I figure he can decide whether to ride with me or return home," said Oumo.

"You never could resist an animal," Davo said before whispering, "Did you get the blessed water?"

"Enough to make the shaman happy." Oumo handed the gourd to Davos.

"What an absurd request: take a gourd of holy water to our people who went with Lord Isha. What are they to do with it?"

"It is not my place to question the shaman's requests," he said.

Davos lowered his voice. "Did you get a good look at the captives?"

"I did, poor souls. No one I recognized. Just as the last time, I saw no women or children among them."

"It's terrible." Davos shuddered. "Death would be better. I found some sympathizers among the guards."

"Well, they should defect and join the resistance," Oumo said, keeping his voice low. "They are cowards."

"As cowardly as my cousin, who is now a member of the palace guard?" Davos ran his fingers through his thinning hair. "We should not complain. The caravan guards protected us from that rogue asura back there. And what about us, Oumo? You're taking produce to the King's kitchens!" Davos berated. "Are we not supporting him as our Lord Isha does?
"

"We support our cousins who are in the palace, Davos. My vegetables feed the palace. If the rumour is true, the King is a carnivore," said Oumo.

"Believe what you must so you can sleep at night, Oumo. These are desperate times," Davos replied.

As the men spoke, Sinha's ears twitched with interest. His tail flicked dangerously back and forth as he digested the information.

Perceiving movement, Sinha's attention snapped to the wagon carrying bushels of vegetables: okra, eggplant, long leeks, and onions. Ropes of dried herbs and garlic hung inside the woven leaf frame. With a leap and scurry, he found his quarry: a sinuous form lying in the cool straw between the hemp sacks.

"Snake!" Oumo's eyes widened in alarm.

Before either brother-husband could react, Sinha sprang into action. Overcome with feline instinct and with unsheathed claws, he cornered the snake. His paws moved in a series of swift strikes, and he herded the long, sand-coloured viper out of the wagon. Weary from the assault, the snake slithered away, hissing its frustration. It gave Sinha a withered look before vanishing into a dune at the edge of the open road.

Sinha blinked warily. The danger had passed. He was victorious.

Breathless with relief, Oumo scooped the cat into his arms. "By the grace of the Gods of our herd, my gratitude to you, cat." Oumo stroked Sinha's head and gave him a scratch behind the ears.

Davos patted Sinha on the head before running to meet Saida, who was leading a long string of water buffalo.

"I honestly don't know what she sees in him, Sinha." Oumo stroked Sinha's head and gave him a scratch behind the ears. "Will you ride with me?"

In answer, Sinha jumped from his arms to the wagon, knocking over a heap of blankets.

The wagon was huge, stocked with sacks and crates, leaving little space for passengers. After a brief exploration, Sinha burrowed into the layer of soft straw mixed with scented herbs spread on the floor, and rolled in its pleasant earthiness. In the quiet and safe space, he let his outer senses take in the village around them.

As Ishwara predicted, there were no demons or asura there. The guards were anxious to leave the village. He received flashes of the sealed well and the righteous anger of the villagers. Sinha yawned with satisfaction. He let his tongue pant in the heat and chuckled to himself. Despite the power the King had amassed, the guards' fear betrayed a singular truth: they feared the wrath of the Greater Gods.

The sun passed its midday mark. A platoon formed a rearguard at the end of the caravan's long train as Oumo and Saida made final preparations for departure. Guards and drivers shouted orders while the line in front of Oumo's wagon waited attentively. Saida had returned with a string of eight water buffalo.

While Oumo and Davos hitched them to the complex yokes that would pull the heavy wagon, she finished checking that nothing attached to the wagon was loose.

She welcomed Sinha with a cautious pat on the head in greeting. He bumped his head into her hand and was rewarded with a smile.

The train started to stumble out of the village. When it was his turn, Oumo gave a solid push to the well-muscled rump of the last water buffalo with his bare foot. The large black bovine started to move.

The beasts' excitement was made apparent by a sudden burst of excrement from their rears. With a jolt, the wagon began to roll through ruts formed in the dried earth cracked from drought. The grass had grown in the middle of the road, fuelled by a steady supply of dung, providing a welcome snack to the beasts.

"Well, we're off, Sinha." Oumo glanced back at Davos, drawing Saida into the back of the wagon. Sinha followed his gaze. "And there they go.

"Come up here to join me."

Sinha stretched before jumping to the raised bench of the driver's seat. He sat regally, watching the vacant houses pass. He did not see Banchic among the villagers.

Oumo let out a long breath of air. "This will be the seventh time I'm travelling to the palace with vegetables. I am glad for your company. The journey can be more than a little unnerving."

No guards were stationed outside the temple. High Priest Mani stood next to Banchic at the gates. The young man was clothed in the herdspeople's uniform of shirt and pants, complete with head covering and travel scarf. He carried a cloth bag and a waterskin.

The priest waved for them to slow down. "Cats are rare in these parts," Mani said. "He rides with you."

"Aye, sir," said Oumo.

"We are short of time. You agreed to provide passage for Banchic," Mani said. Though they moved slowly, the cart before Oumo's, piled high with rolls of cloth, had left a distance the guards would notice.

"Climb up, boy," Oumo said to Banchic. "If anyone asks, you're my son."

Meeting Mani's gaze, he said, "No promises, but we will do our best."

"Ishwara preserve—that is all we can hope for," replied the High Priest. "Thank you, and go with blessings."

Banchic climbed up to join Oumo on the bench and sat in silence as they left the village. Sinha moved to Banchic's lap, hoping to provide a soothing presence. The gentle rocking of the wagon and the breeze introduced through its movement had the two of them nodding off to sleep. Being a cat was nice. Maybe when his mission was over, he could be a cat. He fell asleep to the slow song Oumo crooned in time with their pace:

*In the heart of life's tangled dance,*
*Virtue's song we must enhance.*
*With kindness and truth, our souls align,*
*Guiding us through the paths divine.*

The wagon stopped for the evening at a ford crossing a great river. While in daylight, half of the vehicles and guards crossed to the far embankment. The remainder, including several buffalo wagons, set up camp on the near embankment. Having slept for most of the journey, Sinha and Banchic woke refreshed to find Oumo laying out a short table, which was no more than a raised board.

"Banchic, is there anything you can't eat?" Oumo asked as he laid out the food and drink.

"I eat everything." The boy stumbled down from the wagon to stand next to him.

"We should have enough to feed you." Oumo smiled as he handed Banchic a crate containing small clay pots of stewed lentils and cold pickled vegetables.

As Saida and Davos descended from the wagon, her gaze met Oumo's. She set Davos to task, climbing up the outside of the wagon to haul grass to feed the buffalo. Saida approached with an armload of wood to build a small fire.

"Davos is my wife's second husband. Give him no mind. As the gods did not invite him to our meeting, it's best he remains unaware of Sinha's purpose."

"Can you get us into the palace?" Banchic unpacked the crate.

"I can get you to the palace gates, possibly the kitchens—would that be close enough?" Oumo asked.

"I have something to deliver to the Prince."

"From what I know, the Prince's situation changes daily." Oumo poured an herbal pomegranate tea into four cups.

"Do you know of the prophesy?" Banchic asked. Without being asked, he recited,

*When Ishwara's well is dry,*
*a hero will be nearby.*
*The rightful king enthroned.*
*A new era born.*

*The Greater Gods will rise,*
*sending demons low.*
*The people return to lands*
*of long, long ago.*

"I only know the first line," Oumo whispered. "Has the well gone dry?"

"It has," Banchic said.

"An end to the tyrant king." Oumo sat back on his haunches, beaming, his eyes shining with joy. A single tear fell. He wiped it away. "Our people have been returned to the mortal realm by our Goddess. I will not see them again in this lifetime."

Saida put her arms around him in an embrace. "Sshh . . . Davos returns," she warned. She served them warmed rice porridge in cold dishes and offered Sinha a small bowl to sample.

As he ate his first meal, the seed of knowledge carried within his psyche sprouted. The porridge was a congee of rice, nuts, and dried meat softened in animal stock. He could not say whether it was good or bad, but his belly felt warm afterward.

"You're not afraid to go to the capital?" Davos asked after a brief introduction.

Banchic nodded.

Davos whistled low. "What do you hope to do?"

Sinha watched from the shadows. Davos had accepted Banchic's presence without question, as if it were their habit to give passage to strangers. Saida wore a short spear strapped to her back and was dressed in the same garb as the men. That she was a woman was only apparent up close. She was as taut as a bowstring as she focused on the people around them. When she raised a hand, the men fell silent.

"Enough talk. We are being watched," she whispered through clenched teeth. "There are those among the merchants who would sell their mothers in a heartbeat." She smiled sweetly and spoke in a normal voice, "Banchic, since you're so comfortable in the back of the wagon, how about you sleep with the vegetables? You will not be cold with Sinha and blankets for warmth. Oumo, Davos, and I sleep under the wagon."

"I will manage." Banchic was tense despite his bravado.

"Good. Let's put away all of this. Tomorrow, we have to be ready to travel the moment dawn touches the sky," Saida said.

The wagon was comfortably high for those sleeping underneath on sheets of sweet-smelling braided grass. A cloth was draped to provide privacy. Davos made himself scarce while Oumo and Banchic took the team of water buffalo to the river to drink. Sinha followed and watched as they tethered them in a field set aside for livestock. Under dark skies, more herdspeople joined their little circle, bearing firewood and snacks.

In the flickering darkness of the wagon, Sinha curled up in Banchic's lap as the boy sat and listened to the subdued folk songs and storytelling. Banchic was shy to join, having only the language of his village and the common trade tongue. He made do by burrowing into the straw in the back of the wagon with blankets for warmth.

With Banchic settled, Sinha climbed to the highest vantage point. His senses identified the older men preparing their beds. He watched Saida practicing a complex dance with her staff. Her body contorted and turned. She jumped and twirled as if fighting against an invisible foe. Sinha knew she was avoiding both of her husbands this evening. How she could partner herself with two men who were so opposite was a mystery to him. Then again, he knew nothing of mortal love and relationships.

The vehicles had been parked in a semicircle. The smaller ones were closer to the river, while the larger ones, belonging to the herdspeople, were lined up around the outside. Livestock were tethered within a single field. The vehicles on the other side of the river had been set up in a mirror formation. It looked as though a wagon city nestled on the great river's banks.

While they had dinner, several guards dug a thin gutter, forming a semicircle around the wagon city. Many used this gutter as a toilet.

At dusk, a horn sounded three loud bursts, and the gutter was flooded with water, flushing excrement and waste downstream to reunite with the river. The water continued to flow, providing an unbroken barrier.

Unlike the herdspeople, there was no laughter or song among the groups of merchants. Guards kept themselves separate from everyone else as if friendship were a path to betrayal. The caravan—where there was only fear and distrust—was in stark contrast to the love and protectiveness Sinha had witnessed in the village.

By sundown, two robed men accompanied by guards walked out to the cardinal points on the inside of the water channel. One intoned a note and rang a bell while the other waved his hands and hit the ground with his staff. Energy unfolded and converged into a concave shield. The shields were anchored to standing stones buried deep at the cardinal points, following the gutters to the river. Sinha's knowledge filled in the blanks: the shield would hold until dawn broke, serving as a barrier to all living things. While, as a cat, he could not cross the shield, he could sense an eddy of energies building outside of it.

Darkness fell. Shadows awoke. Demons roamed. Sinha's hair rose with a positive charge. Now he understood why the caravan had travelled together despite their discord. It was unsafe to be alone on these roads or in these lands. Lightning flashed overhead.

"Lion-cat? Sinha?" Banchic's voice held dread and fear.

Reading his worries, Sinha settled himself next to Banchic. Alone and away from his village for the first time, he kept vigil as the young man's faith wavered in the press of darkness and flashing lights surrounding them.

Banchic spoke to him of missing his mother, who would also be alone without him. No, the neighbours would watch out for her. She would be safe. He regretted his bravado. Who was he to join the rebellion? He could not even fight.

Beyond the shields were things that craved and feasted on fear. Sinha projected calm. *The Greater Gods chose you, Banchic. You are where you need to be. I am here to guard you.*

Although Banchic could not hear him, he settled, and his breathing slowed as he fell asleep.

Sinha sensed the malevolent intentions of Demons travelling across the night sky. He picked his way back to the driver's seat and counted the dark shadows passing overhead from which no light could penetrate. Cloud formations moved erratically. At times, a burst of light or a rainbow passed. A shooting star moved too close to be of celestial origin, momentarily flooding the wagon village with light. The shields held. Sinha remained undetected by the warring spirits above as he kept watch over his small group of humans.

Before dawn, Sinha woke to the sound of Oumo using coals from the fire to bake flatbread and boil a kettle of water for tea. Banchic voiced appreciation for the hot bread to warm their cold hands and fill their grumbling bellies as the train began to move.

The second day was uneventful. After a sleepless night, the wagon's sway rocked Sinha to sleep while Oumo crooned twelve verses of his wagon song. By midday, he was joined by Banchic.

"You make it hard for me to stay awake. Your song is a spell."

"The song serves to fill the time. It keeps my mind sharp," Oumo said.

"We have a similar tradition."

The road wound around a rocky outcrop surrounded by grassland. Oumo put his arm around Banchic, drawing him closer as he pointed out the growing city marked by turrets and towers in the far distance. As they rode, the city proved vast, spreading across the horizon.

## A Lion's Head

"Olu, my sister is a cook in the palace kitchens," Oumo said. "She will receive my goods."

"She could get something to the Prince?" Banchic whispered.

"She might," the older man replied.

Banchic went silent, buried in his thoughts. He bit his lip.

"It's holy water," Banchic finally blurted. "Special water. C-ca—" He stuttered.

"Can you trust Olu? You can," Oumo said.

"The palace is dangerous. A young man like you—what's to stop them from taking you from me? I can do naught. That's why I'm happy Saida has Davos should anything happen to me. His being lame . . . those prejudiced fools won't drag him off to the guard."

"Ishwara will preserve," Banchic said.

Saida joined them on the bench. "You have much faith for a young one."

"There's no future without faith," Banchic countered. He pulled on a leather thong from around his neck, revealing a small wax-stoppered glass bottle. "This is what I need to get to the Prince."

*I will take it to him.* Sinha told Oumo.

"Sinha can take it to the Prince," Oumo said. "His mission goes deeper into the palace than the likes of us can tread."

Sinha meowed and set his forepaws on Banchic. He bit the thong to try to lift the bottle from Banchic's hand, with little success. Banchic took a moment to knot the cord around the bottle, forming a protective net.

"There. Now you can pick it up from all sides, and the leather protects the bottle. Think you can keep this safe?"

Sinha picked up the bottle and carried it to the back of the wagon where he hid it near the back gate.

---

Sinha had been innocent, naïve, and trusting on the wagon ride to the palace, seated in the sun next to Oumo. He adored being a cat. He belonged. The comforting rocking of the wagon and falling asleep to Oumo's song.

One day was one hundred years in the mortal realm. Sinha wished he could remain by Oumo's side forever.

After his death, Oumo's spirit had returned to the mortal realm.

Sinha felt pain as his bones reknit and internalized stones were expelled from his form. To escape the physical pain, his consciousness sought Oumo.

Oumo was a butterfly. In the blink of an eye, Oumo was a deer.

He winced, feeling his body flex as it straightened broken bones.

Oumo was a young boy born to a family of hunters. Were these the people of the Water Buffalo Herd? Had the people of the herd survived? Oumo, the hunter, grew to adulthood, married, had children, and lived to an old age.

Sinha watched, celebrating and cheering Oumo's achievements, feeling sadness when Oumo felt a loss.

*Does Oumo know that I watched? Would he know me if we met again?*

The physical pain receded, replaced with overwhelming loneliness.

What was he? He was not a man. He was not a lion. He was not of the asura.

He was invincible . . . for what? To spend eternity with whom?

For the first time in his life, Sinha cried. He could not open his mouth. His body shook with his sobs. Debris shifted and settled around him.

No one would come for him.

# 9

"Something strange is going on," Isha said. He dared not meet the King's eyes. Head bowed, he stared into the scrying bowl. Had Chala suspected he'd used their herd as the King's eyes and ears? He would not have reported on *his* people's doings. Not everyone met the necessary conditioned to be used.

Isha's view through Davos's eyes revealed a handsome cat seated on the wagon bench next to Oumo. They were several days away from the capital. Was Oumo speaking with the cat?

"Katora's well is dry. I wonder who is the hero that is nearby?" he ruminated.

"Don't you mean, where are the Greater Gods?" the King asked. He paced the war room. "Perhaps they have gone the same direction as your herd."

Isha bit his tongue. The metallic taste provided a distraction from the tension creeping down his back.

"My herd is misplaced, Sire," he said. "Are *you* aware of their whereabouts?"

"It was not me, that's for sure, Isha." Hiranyakshipu laughed. "I am unsure whether I should be angry or sympathize with you. I hear your lady left you without saying goodbye."

How much did he know? Did he know there were no provisions for the army? Isha shut down his thoughts too late.

"About those provisions," the King said, "have no worries, Isha. Demons need a different type of provision." He patted Isha on the shoulder. "I was biding my time. Maintaining an army of humans takes too many resources. I want the humans gone from this realm. Your wife has done me a favour."

Isha could not hide his self-serving relief. He felt the tension between his shoulders relax.

"I wonder how I should repay her." The King's smile spoke volumes.

The tension returned to Isha's shoulders.

Hiranyakshipu's eyes twinkled; Isha's misfortune was his pleasure. He sat upon his throne, his gaze focused on Isha. "So, what is your plan for finding your herd? I assume you will want retribution."

"There is time. I will find them." Isha pushed his thoughts to the back of his mind. The King was playing with him. He treated the missing humans the same as Isha would have once thought of a few thousand flies in the mortal realm. Isha felt the rage within kindled by the King's words. Powerless, he gave in to what could only be his curse.

"Perhaps the remaining humans in my army could be coerced into tilling the fields in the lands that were once yours," the King continued.

"As you wish, Your Highness." Noting the King's choice of words, Isha bowed his head lower.

"I also think it's time we tested your men."

Isha's heart caught in his throat. "Sire?"

"Your guard captain and his insignificant band of warriors—let's send them to Anuhlada to see what they are made of."

"Sire, Prince Anuhlada heads the demon horde."

"Exactly."

Isha spoke with a confidence he did not feel. "I ask for time. Let my remaining people investigate the whereabouts of my herd."

"Of course." The King dismissed him with a wave. They were all pawns, subject to the will of the God King.

Isha left the war room with slow and steady steps. He was having trouble breathing under the God King's yoke.

*What would Chala do?*

He gathered his wits and asked Channa to assemble his people. He needed a means to keep them useful and away from the King. Where else was there a need for good men? Where could he shelter his people?

Prince Bashkala found him pacing in his quarters. The shortest and broadest of the King's offspring, Bashkala was also the youngest, dressed in maroon robes embroidered with white cherry blossoms. Serving as his father's herald, the boy had a talent for handing the work of maintaining order to more qualified advisors. In Isha's opinion, he was under-utilized by the King. Maybe that was Bashkala's desire. Though Isha had been the king's favourite, he and Bashkala shared a political truce.

"Have you come to gloat?" Isha asked.

"I come with a proposition," Bashkala said. "Your people serve in positions from cook to guard. Give them over to serve my brother, Prahlada. With so many of his followers joining the rebellion, Father needs neutral people around him. This will send a message to the rebels that he is well cared for."

"What makes you think your father will agree to this?" Isha knew only too well of

King Hiranyakshipu's recent attempt at filicide.

Bashkala strode over to Isha's table to admire his reflection in the polished black stone. He straightened his collar and dusted his shoulders before raising his gaze to meet Isha's. "My father allows your people to worship you. Do you know how unique that is among the asura? No one else is allowed to have followers under his reign."

"Your father desires to be worshipped by the asura, not by mere mortals," Isha replied.

There was nothing else in the room for Bashkala to inspect. He walked to the window to gaze at the courtyard where Isha's herd trained. "Exactly, yours is not the same religion as Prahlada's fanatics," said Bashkala. "Don't forget, Father needs your ability to grow things and change the landscape. You are, as yet, his favourite, Lord Isha."

"Favourite plaything, more like," Isha scoffed.

"A favourite is a favourite," Bashkala admonished. "He has yet to tire of the game he plays with you."

"Why are you offering to help me? What's in it for you?" Isha asked.

## A Lion's Head

Bashkala smiled. *No answers, then? What will he gain from this endeavour? A distraction, maybe. If the King is busy with me, he ignores his children.*

"Take it or leave it, Isha Sura. I hate to see you go the way of so many asura before you," he said.

"I will owe you a favour, then."

"Indeed." Bashkala hesitated at the door. "Isha Sura, did you see anything strange in Katora yesterday?"

"I saw a cat fight a snake."

"Did the cat win?" he asked.

"It did."

"Interesting."

"Be at peace. You owe me nothing. I will arrange everything for your people." Bashkala left before Isha could second-guess his intent.

Relief led to sorrow. He was alone in his yoke, dependent on others. He turned his back to the door. The moss-green wall was all he had left of her.

*What are your secrets?*

Reassembling the wall had not broken its magic. The black earthstone had vanished with his people. Draining the energy of the ceremonial chambers had collapsed the room in on itself. Demolition had felt good. Isha had absorbed the energy into himself, building a mental labyrinth to suppress the madness threatening to overwhelm him. From this same pool, he drew energy to scry his people. He could not overhear their words unless they were near a water buffalo. Lucky for him, his people were never far from their herd beasts.

Davos would make a helpful spy in the King's court. Through Davos's eyes, he could recreate the vision that ended with the cat encountering the snake. He paused as Oumo said, "We support our brothers who are held hostage in the palace, Davos."

Was that where Chala and the herd's perception had strayed from his? True, he was a hostage, held against his will—had he been wrong to keep her in the dark? Maybe if he had told her of the danger, she would have included him in her escape.

She could have told him.

She must not have trusted him.

She was not wrong.

Had the love and life they'd shared for thousands of years been false? When had she stopped loving him? When had she stopped trusting him?

She had wanted him to choose the herd—why had he chosen the God King at that moment? Was this the King's doing?

Anger rose—am I angry at Chala or the King?

"I am free to decide," Isha muttered, "I am in control."

If found, what would the God King do to his wayward lady and his herd? Would it serve their needs to find them?

The King had bound millions of mortals to his army. The coercion was subtle. The King could strip his herd of all free will and enslave them. How much had he contributed to the God King's successes? His people were in even greater danger than they were in before.

A moan of despair escaped his lips.

*I am alone.*

He locked the door as another moan threatened to escape.

*Alone. Abandoned . . . unloved.*

*I am half of a whole.*

He paced the length of the wall, stopping when he realized the words in the moss wall had changed:

> *Find strength. Gather together.*
> *The hero's time will come.*

*The green moss will be the cure.*
*When the act is done.*

For a long time, he wondered, *Am I the hero? Will this be my time?*

# 10

A day later, Isha received an invitation to attend the King's War Council.

True to his word, Bashkhala had installed Channa and his men as honour guards for the King's eldest son, Prince Prahlada. He had gone as far as to convince his father this was a good idea.

Prahlada was a virtuous man with an unshakable faith in the Greater Gods; however, his fanatics' vitriol was a cancer on the King's reign. Rumours of filicide fuelled the rebellion. Would-be prophets named Prahlada the King's successor.

Hiranyakshipu would never step aside. He was said to be invincible, which was tantamount to being immortal.

The Prince's record for keeping servants was poor. His enraged father often dismissed or killed his household outright. As was the case of Lady Holika, the King showed little remorse for his actions. Bystanders lost their lives while those two remained standing.

Prahlada was neither Isha's friend nor his ally.

Isha noted the courtier's whispers. Their buzz reminded him of the days his ears had been privy to the messages of the flies and bees. He swallowed to bury the memory deep as it threatened to sway his composure.

He walked with his head held high, his gaze straight ahead. The entire distance from his rooms to the war chamber felt as though he were walking on coals. The King respected those who were arrogant and held their ground—Isha could not afford to show weakness.

The tall wooden pillars holding the roof stood as silent sentinels. He paused as a breeze brought the smell of grass through the open walkway, allowing himself a scant moment to inhale and relax. He would survive this challenge. Maybe the green moss wall would reveal its secrets and tell him where Chala was.

With hope lightening his footsteps, he entered the war chamber.

"Father, you are a formidable foe," simpered Bash.

Isha followed the King's lead and ignored him. "Ishwara's well was sealed several days ago," Isha reported. "I have not seen or heard anything untoward since."

"The well runs dry, and a hero is nearby," the King sang. "Perhaps the hero will meet me on the battlefield."

"They will be defeated," Bash said, "Lord Father!"

"Call in my sons," the King commanded.

"Lord, they sent in their reports. Anuhlada leads the battle against Indra's armies. Samhlada reported drought, poor harvest, hunger, and starvation. The human population is in steady decline. We have been unable to reclaim the lands claimed by the rogue Kraken. Hlada has been turned away from negotiations with the naga beings. Shibi is investigating rumours of stargates in the mountains." Bashkala recited while Isha prepared his spell.

In his experience, it was best to do as the King asked, even if it wasted time and energy. Not seeing his children daily, the King's paranoia would paint them all conspirators, fools, or worse. Isha's summoning spell was a blinding verdurous whirlwind that whipped loose clothing and hair. As it reached its end, it revealed a group of four armoured asura. "They are summoned," Isha replied, ignoring the distress of those summoned. He did not care for their failures or successes as long as his people were safe.

"Maha Isha Sura, what is the meaning of this? Do you hope we will lose the war?" The angriest and mightiest of those summoned, the giant Anuhlada, was dressed in a silver and white military uniform. His war-mask, a grotesque caricature of his father's face, hung from a thong around his neck. Having appeared with his back to his father, he stood two heads taller than Hiranyakshipu, his face contorted with annoyance. His eyes widened with comprehension at seeing Isha's nod. He turned about face to bow low to his father, his expression as grim as his mask.

"Report on your progress, Anuhlada," the King said, maintaining an outward appearance of boredom.

"There is no progress. Send me back, and I will give you progress," Anuhlada replied. He had a reputation for limited patience, feeding into an aggressiveness on which his father preyed.

"Indra's armies can wait. Our forces are greater than his. We will overrun them soon," his father replied. "Report."

"Father, we have Indra surrounded. I was about to give the command to attack."

The King listened to some unseen voice. "Indra has withdrawn; what you were seeing was an illusion. How can you be so blind?"

"I can only speak from my experience, Father."

"Unleash our demons. They will have no constraints when whittling them down."

"The demons hold no value to life, Father. They are as apt to lay destruction to our forces as those of the enemy. I would prefer to hold them back," Anuhlada countered.

"That shouldn't stop you. Use them—they are my best weapons," the King commanded. "We are paying dearly for them. Must I feed them our armies when they could be feeding on our enemies?"

Anuhlada punched a pillar. It splintered and broke in two. Shale and dust from the roof rained down on them.

"Lord, what makes our reports inadequate?" the grey-robed Hlada asked.

"How many times must I tell you this: I need you present when you report."

"But Lord, what does the rebellion have to do with the warfront?" Shibi asked. "How does this relate to my negotiations with the demi-gods or Hlada's work finding stargates?
"

"Why is this so hard to understand? What good are reports when none of you communicate with each other?" Hiranyakshipu's temper flared. "Set the realm on fire! I should not have to tell you what to do! You should know what to do!"

The brown-robed Samhlada dropped to one knee. "Lord Father, I don't have enough asura to conquer the disputed territories," he said. "We're dealing with a new rebellion in lands that have always been ours."

"What I'm seeing is that you are not capable or willing to put in the hard work," the King said. "Samhlada, you can be replaced. Had I put a demon in charge, the rebellion would be over. You waste time with your politics."

"Is that so, Father?" Samhlada replied.

The King rose. "Enslave the minor demons... and the mortals."

"Lord, that will not be acceptable to our allies," Shibi exclaimed. "We would be creating one more problem without solving the first."

"The enslaved troops must be subdued and controlled. We do not have enough resources," Samhlada said.

"Lord." Hlada stood behind Samhlada, keeping his gaze to the ground.

The King's voice was dangerously quiet. "The demi-gods don't need to know."

"Just get the job done. Incompetent is what I say you are. My brother and I conquered this realm–just the two of us."

The slow clap of Anuhlada's hands drew everyone's attention as he feigned laughter. "You inherited the realm from our uncle."

"Do you think it was easy? Do you think I wanted this?" the King shouted. He grew in size in preparation to strike Anuhlada, pausing with his hand mid-air, seeing his son's armour. Instead, he took Anuhlada's war-mask between his hands, and gazed into the fearsome eyes of the face. He said, "I will avenge the killing of my brother and finish what he started."

"And what is that, Lord Father?" Anuhlada asked.

"To be the only God in the universe."

Isha did not have to look around the room to see the looks on the princes' faces. The King was mad. He could feel the madness black and palpable, connecting him to the King's aura. "My Lord, Ishwara's well has run dry." He spoke quietly to break the impasse.

The King chuckled. His chuckle grew into a laugh. "I will call out my foes once and for all!" He laughed again. "You are dismissed."

"Come, Isha, my buffalo brother—I can smell the noon-time meal roasting." He threw his arm around Isha.

---

Bashkala held up his hand to stop his brothers as they began to leave.

"I am so tired of this," Hlada said. "He sows chaos while keeping us running on an infinite wheel. How am I to negotiate with demi-gods, who can tell the truth from a lie?"

"You won't," Bashkala said, patting his shoulder.

"At this rate, there will be nothing left to rule," Shibi replied. "He has no idea what he is asking. Once the mortals die out, this realm will be a hell. Are we to use the stargates to escape? What use are they to Maha Isha Sura's people? Father is purposely keeping that minotaur in the dark."

"Don't be a fool. He plans to unleash the demons on the other realms," Bashkala said. "Isha Sura reminds father of our uncle, Hiranyaksha. He is the nearest thing he has to a friend, if you could call it that. Master and pawn, more like."

"Father is making my life impossible. He is not the one negotiating with demons. They create more casualties than our enemies," Anuhlada said.

Bashkala raised his palm, calling for silence among his brothers.

"You all need to know—the Greater Gods have withdrawn," Bashkala said. "Samhlada, have the rebels also retreated?"

"They have gone underground," Samhlada replied quietly. "Enslave the minor demons and humans—tsk . . . what is he thinking?"

"Brothers, it's all smoke and mirrors. Just give Father the answer he wants. I agree with Anuhlada: he does not know what he is doing."

"Whoever granted him the boon of invincibility was daft. He destroys everything out of boredom because he can," Bashkala said. "Only Prahlada's faith stands in his way."

"You all know we play along with this farce until our brother is free," Anuhlada said.

"Shh . . . bide your time until our brother's time comes," Bashkala whispered. "Prahlada willed it."

"While father is in power, to fail is treason. I, for one, am happy to admit I was wrong," Samhlada added. "If the well has gone dry, it may be time for us to unmask our allegiance. Hold off on his orders. The Greater Gods have withdrawn. To make the wrong move now would be to go against the heavens."

"Prahlada's time is near?" Anuhlada let out a long breath. "But, Father is . . . invincible."

"All that matters is our brother will no longer be a hostage, I trust the Gods must have a plan," Samhlada said. "I pray for the day to be upon us so that we can be free."

# 11

Curiosity drew Sinha to investigate Oumo's irritation.

"Inauspicious . . . inauthentic . . . impertinent . . ." Oumo muttered.

*All words that begin with the sound "ih?"* Sinha offered. He looked down at Oumo from his perch beside Banchic, who was securing the upper-storey ropes. Leaping, he landed, with a thud, next to Oumo.

"Davos clings to her as if she is his property . . . and she lets him. She, a woman ten years his senior!" Sweat formed on Oumo's temples as he leaned on his haunches and worked the heavy block out from under the wagon wheel. "Now the freeloader sits with a headache while there is work to be done . . . and she does his share!"

Sinha chose not to give Oumo the reason for Davos's exhaustion. His instincts told him that knowledge would do more harm than good. Instead, he sat listening, shaking the inertia from his paws. When his friend's rant slowed, he touched his nose to Oumo's. A faint spark of electricity travelled through the touch.

Oumo sat back on his haunches. "No point working myself up, is there, Sinha?" he said. "I know nothing of him. I was roaming the world long before he was born. She made her choice. She's an adult and a warrior at that. She can fight this battle when she chooses."

*You miss having your wife to yourself.* Perhaps the truth would help Oumo see reason. *She is infatuated with Davos but carries a deep love for you.*

Oumo gave Sinha a stern look.

The Truth did not help?

Guards gathered at the rear and front of the caravan train as the time for departure approached. With oxen drivers shouting and clicking their tongues, the line in front of the wagon was being readied. Oumo continued to yoke the buffalo and pull the last anchors from under the eight wheels.

Meanwhile, Davos sat with his arm around Saida's waist, as she tried to pull away—her discomfort palpable.

Her mixed intentions were impossible to read. Sinha took Oumo's words to heart.

*She is a grown woman; let her fight her own battles.*

"Is that how you treat your elder in public?" Banchic's shrill, outraged voice startled Sinha and Oumo, who, dumbfounded, could only watch the exchange between the two younger men.

"She's no relation to you." Davos glared at Banchic, who stood between the two lovers.

"I heard her ask you to stop. Are you blind and deaf to her discomfort? Did no one teach you respect?"

"Are you offering, boy?" Davos sneered.

"Banchic, it's all right," Saida answered through gritted teeth, her face flush with shame.

"It is not right."

"This is none of your affair," Davos shoved Banchic aside and took Saida's hand, dragging her into the darkness of the wagon's interior.

"Why does she tolerate him?" Banchic exclaimed to no one in particular. He sat down, absently stroking Sinha. "Isn't she supposed to be a warrior or something?" he muttered. "I don't understand."

Oumo's jealousy of Davos evaporated, replaced with shame.

"Infatuation, right?" he said, glaring at the cat. "Maybe I should have a word with her."

*Truth be told, she is conflicted. As I am new to you, he is new to her.* Sinha said, *We all become old with time.*

"I'm the old man, huh?" Oumo said, and Banchic gave him an exasperated look that said, "Daft old man, talking to himself."

Sinha sat with his regret. *I apologize. I am not used to conversing.*

"What *are* you used to?" Oumo said. His face contorted in response to the wave of flatulence from the straining beasts.

"Not this!" Banchic gave a whoop of disgust and climbed up to a seat he had fashioned out of firewood. Oumo glanced at him with a twinkle in his eyes and a shake of his head that said "Youth".

*Everything is new to me.*

Sinha wondered how the train of carts got anywhere. Tall, lush, untouched patches of grass were discovered by the hungry buffalo who paused to graze as the wagons began their slow forward motion.

"What are you, Sinha?" Oumo whispered.

*A construct. The Greater Gods, Ishwara, Sakka, and Surya, created me. I am a cat for now. When it is time, I will become my true self.*

"Sinha, the man-lion," Oumo said. "A mighty hero like Varaha who defeated Hiranyaksha. Why the gods think to create a man-animal hybrid every time is beyond me."

*It has more to do with how asura are in the habit of collecting riddles of invincibility.* Sinha said.

Oumo whistled low. The water buffalo perked their ears to their master in anticipation as they began to cross the ford.

Crossing the river captivated Sinha. Its opalescent surface reflected the colour and light of the sky. The buffalo splashed as they broke the surface, breaking the image into a thousand ripples.

"So that's it. *He* can't be killed by a normal man or something like that," Oumo said. "Bet a woman could get the job done."

*Unfortunately, not in this instance*, Sinha replied, *Here is the riddle:*

> *Death cannot be experienced by him,*
> *while the sun or moon crosses the sky,*
> *when he is inside or outside a dwelling,*
> *while in the air or touching earth,*
> *in the heavens or in the hells.*
> *No weapon, palm, or fist can kill him—*
> *borne by human, deity, demon, or animal.*

"Lord and Lady of the herd—that's steep. I'm glad they created you for the job." Oumo whispered, "You're no deity, and no one knows you exist except us."

The landscape changed after crossing the river ford. The once-barren landscape gave way to patches of grass and boulders. The road angled upward, climbing small hills. Sinha spotted scraggly trees braving the constant wind. The smell of crushed grass, wet buffalo, and dung permeated the air.

"You seem knowledgeable," Oumo said before clicking his tongue to signal for the water buffalo to increase their speed.

*I know things, but only when I need to. I know things about the universe. What I know about mortals is limited.* Sinha replied.

"Is that why you're with us?"

*To learn about you, yes. To experience your life, I suppose. I am an egg waiting to hatch. While I don't exist, I might as well enjoy it.* Sinha replied.

"You're talking to the cat, old man," Banchic called from his perch. "What's he saying?"

"You will have to come down if you want a part of this, young man," Oumo said. "The wind is picking up. We're upwind of my four-legged brothers. Your sensitive nose is safe."

## A Lion's Head

Banchic scrambled down, bumping into Saida, causing her to stumble out of the wagon's interior. Her gaze met that of Banchic and Oumo, who turned away as she blushed.

"He sleeps," she said.

Sinha read what went unspoken. Not wanting relations with Davos, she had knocked him unconscious. He had no experience in human relationships to understand her actions, so the mystery gnawed at him. Exposing her secret was out of the question. He chose to sit in her lap to calm her frayed nerves.

"Oumo was about to tell me what our hero, Sinha, is saying to him," Banchic began.

"I believe you," she said, her gaze meeting Oumo's and then falling to Sinha. "We four are together for a reason."

With the practice of a herd storyteller, Oumo repeated what Sinha had told him and Hiranyakshipu's riddle of immortality verbatim. The three sat silently while the water buffalo pulled the wagon higher into the foothills toward their destination.

"You would have to hit him at dusk for neither sun nor moon to be in the sky," Banchic said after a time.

"Bring the roof down—that's how a person can be both inside and outside a dwelling at the same time," Oumo said, "Most of the palace buildings have an open design—Sinha, are you strong enough to break a stone column?"

*I don't know.*

"If you are able to carry him, he will be both off the ground and not in the air at the same time. If you can use your knee, like so, and crack." Saida sat on one knee and mimed breaking a stick of tinder over her exposed knee. "If you can draw from infinite strength and catch him by complete surprise, that is. He is known to be a formidable warrior. If he suspects you, he will end you before you get close."

Her words elicited braying laughter from Banchic. Soon, they were all laughing. Sinha cocked his head. Their behaviour was strange. In their hearts, they were terrified. Yet, they laughed. They laughed through the fear. He was enveloped in their budding hope that everything would work out, paired with the fear they would all die in the attempt.

"In the heavens or in the hells—our very existence in this realm proves it to be neither," Oumo said. "I'm beginning to understand why he has a problem with mortals being in this realm."

"What of the line about the weapon?" Banchic whispered.

"No weapon, palm, or fist can kill him," Oumo recited.

*That one will be easy. No worries. I am a man-lion. I will have claws.*

"You're going to scratch him to death?" Oumo asked with the naivety of a pacifist.

In response, Sinha gave him a blank stare.

"Oumo, if he is a man-lion created by the Gods. Surely, his form will have deadly claws," Saida said.

*I am an instrument of death. Or, I will be.* Sinha chirped.

"He's so cute!" Banchic picked up Sinha and hugged him.

A leaf of truth unfolded in Sinha's mind, ruining the feline pleasure he received from being held by Banchic—if Hiranyakshipu succeeded in overrunning the mortal realm with demons, he would become invincible in all known realms of the universe. The outcome was not one Sinha wished for the humans. He would protect them in this life or the next.

The wagon rolled to a stop outside the gates of the capital. A stone fortification seven storeys high towered over them. Sinha lay dormant, ears at attention. Oumo sang his song in a low, monotonous voice—more to calm his nerves and those of the water buffalo than to entertain.

Saida embraced Banchic, holding his head to her shoulder. "Everything will be alright," she whispered. "You will feel fear like you never have before. Don't panic. I am here. Everything will be all right." She repeated this mantra until they were clear of the gates.

The city guards, low-level asura, paid no attention to the mortals as they inspected the wagon and waved Oumo forward. The acrid smell of brimstone made Sinha sneeze as they passed under the gate.

Two ugly stone gargoyles were perched above the gates. To look up was to see a pair of terrifying red glowing eyes. The demons were so dark they absorbed all light and colour. With greed, they extracted their toll to pass through the gates.

Davos, in the back of the wagon, screamed.

"Should we have left Davos alone?" Oumo asked, "He has never experienced this."

"He sleeps," Saida replied through her teeth.

Banchic clung to her. "Is it over yet?" he asked.

Saida had chosen to protect Banchic from the demon-induced fear, but Davos was not safe. Drawing the attention of the monsters, Davos would be marked—in this life and the next.

The knowledge came unasked. Sinha said nothing out of caution.

He found Davos whimpering in his sleep, curled in a fetal position. Sinha curled up as close to the man's midsection as he could. He hoped his presence would be enough. The King harnessed his demons by preying on the weak, but Sinha felt no fear and passed under them undetected.

When Oumo dismounted and led his obstinate beasts forward on foot, Sinha felt it was safe to return to his perch on the driver's seat.

For several hours, the large wagons had slowed to the speed of traffic on city streets populated by carts, beasts, single riders, and pedestrians.

Saida and Banchic spoke in low tones of how the kingdom's people attended to their business and lived in a hierarchical society oblivious to the hardship and rebellion beyond its gates.

They were made to wait while the captives accompanying the caravan were separated and sorted in what appeared to be a large paved square. With so many people, immortals and mortals, converged in one place, Sinha kept himself out of sight.

The city guards were asura with a strong sense of duty born out of the desire to support their families and advance their ranks. Sinha sensed no ill will among the citizens. There was no fear of the guard as there had been in the village. Asura men and women held ambition, hope, love, and heartbreak. Cocooned in their walled city, they had all they needed. The inhabitants were willing prisoners—oblivious to the martial law under which they were ruled.

Humans were kept as servants or slaves. This general acceptance of the way things were puzzled Sinha. His righteous anger flared, seeing the enslavement of the mortals, yet their captors were not of ill intent. These were acceptable social norms. Sinha spent the rest of the journey trying to digest the information.

## A Lion's Head

The caravan proceeded through the capital's main streets with merchant and herd wagons parting ways to go up or down forks in the main throughway. As the road was less busy, Oumo returned to the driver's seat.

*Where do they go?*

"Their supplies will find those in need within the city."

*Is it safe?*

"I have rejoined them every time without fail. Let's hope this time is like the last—Lady Chala, guide me," Oumo said, petting Sinha's head absently. "In this life or the next."

By nightfall, the wagon still continued along the main thoroughfare. They had been stopped at several checkpoints and were allowed to continue each time after showing a clay chit to the attending guard. The closer they came to the palace, the cleaner, emptier, and broader the streets became. Shops took up the first floors of buildings, replacing rickety stalls. They passed gated gardens and tall stone and wood palisades, housing the wealthy and elite.

Finally, they were one of six wagons stopped at the city's heart. Stone walls, three storeys in height and as thick as a wagon, served as a barricade between the palace and the city. Raised bonfires lit the entrance, sending sparks and smoke into the dark sky. This time, mauve-clad palace guards stopped the wagon for a final and more thorough inspection. The guards were the first asura to interact with them. Given their bearing, they did not care for humans.

Sinha hid between the sacks of vegetables at the back of the wagon, Banchic's bottle containing Katora's holy water in his mouth at the ready. His heart raced with excitement. Several guards held torches up to inspect the inside of the wagon. He was grateful for the low flickering light and his gold and tawny camouflage.

Sinha heard the shallow breathing of an asura dressed in rich robes of ebony satin beaded with gems. He was tall and wore the head of a water buffalo on the body of a man. The asura was tall enough to stand head-to-head with Oumo seated high up in the driver's seat of the wagon. He peered at Oumo with intense, beady eyes; his face was dark, with a long snout ending in a smooth, black, leathery nose. His white horns were like brightly shining crescent moons drawn outwards from behind his short bovine ears.

"Your Lordship, Isha Sura! We are blessed to be met by you," Oumo said. He dipped his head low with reverence.

"Elder Oumo of my herd, good evening to you." Though his words were polite, the asura seemed impatient.

"Lord, I am so grateful to find you well. I am honoured. I am fortunate to be met by you." Oumo held his head high and sniffed loudly as part of his response.

The asura sniffed the air, and his eyes narrowed. "What do you bring with you, Oumo?"

"Just vegetables, My Lord."

The bull-headed god placed his hands to either side of Oumo's arms and lifted the man down from the wagon, while sniffing his shirt and body.

"Now, hear now! Great Lord, there's no need for this! I am happy to get down if that is what you ask of me," shouted Oumo with the indignation of an elder. "I am of the herd!"

"Lord Isha Sura, please put my husband down," Saida said. She climbed down from the wagon, followed by Banchic. The asura guards had stopped their search to note the exchange.

"You did not go with Chala?" Isha Sura asked.

"I did not."

Isha Sura's composure wavered with her reply. He gazed at her for a long moment before turning his attention to Banchic. "A Katoran."

"He is my adopted son, Banchic," Oumo professed.

"—and a cat . . . where is it? I can smell it." Isha wrinkled his nose and sniffed the top of Saida and Banchic's heads.

"My love of animals is widely known, Lord. What harm have I done?" asked Oumo, who sat on his haunches and prostrated himself.

"Are you aware Lady Chala vanished with the herd several days ago?" Isha Sura asked them.

"Aye, Lord Isha," Saida met his gaze. "How are you taking her absence?"

"Sir," Oumo interrupted, "we chose to remain with you. We also brought Davos to serve you."

The water buffalo-headed asura grunted with what could only be exasperation.

"Guards, continue your search of the wagon. The rest of you come with me," Isha said.

"This one is ill," the guard called from inside the wagon. He returned carrying Davos over his shoulder. "Also, what of the beasts?"

## A Lion's Head

Sinha chose that moment to jump down from the back of the wagon. Determined to keep his promise, he carried the bottle of holy water in his mouth. He waited behind the wagon's wheels until the asura guards began their search inside the wagon. They dumped the vegetables from their sacks. As squashes and eggplants fell to the ground, Sinha dashed across the stone-paved courtyard into the palace gardens. He did not stop running until he found cover under a large flowering shrub. His body shook with adrenaline.

He waited there for his heart to slow. He sat under the bush for a time. Sensing no immediate threat, he stretched each limb and neck by arching his back. He dared not worry about Oumo, Saida, and Banchic's fate. He trusted the Gods to protect them. The best-laid plans were meant to be broken. For the time being, he was a cat, so he would play the part of a cat. How had the asura known he was with Oumo?

He dug a hole to secure the bottle against the shrub's trunk. It could stay there until he found his way to the Prince.

The palace consisted of a series of large rectangular buildings. The gardens were ornate, with empty ponds and fountains to cool the hot climate. Black and gold banners and life-sized bronze castings of the King were everywhere.

At this late hour, dozens of servants cleaned and polished. He passed unnoticed by moving in the shadows. A gilded throne and cushioned seats sat at the ready for the King and his council. Green copper lamps hung from the rafters. Tall bronze oil lamps were spaced at regular intervals across the floor—plenty of places for an orange cat to hide. Sinha made himself small, his colouring a natural camouflage against the bronze and the golden lights. He found the dining pavilion by following his nose.

Sinha paused to listen to the harsh laughter and loud discourse. A slew of emotions fractured his senses: hatred for mortals, disgust for rebels, envy for one another. A resplendent dark-haired man dressed in golden robes laughed as he dined.

*The Asura King Hiranyakshipu.*

The King's dark, distrusting gaze weighted down those assembled. His party sat on a raised dais. A line of servants passed dishes and pitchers of drink from one to the next. Sinha smelled cooked and raw meats, bread, and heavily spiced vegetables. Once the King had been served, dishes were placed in the shared space available to those seated. The dishes were passed down the line until those at the farthest end of the table were left with only the scraps. From there, someone whisked away the empty dish. The most important person in attendance sat closest to the King.

Prince Prahlada would not be there.

He was stumped. Where were they hiding the Prince?

He would have to try his luck in the kitchens with Olu, the herdspeople's cook.

# 12

Isha Sura was not accustomed to making mistakes.

He had clout over the guards, but they were not his men. The stupid asura guards had taken his orders at face value. They were dismantling the wagon and its contents, much to Oumo and Saida's distress. At least, the water buffalo had been led to the stables.

Davos was in bad shape after receiving a demon's touch. What else could go wrong? He did not have Chala's gift for healing. Davos was better off dead than suffering through the drawn-out draining of his life force. His skin had turned red and blistered from the heat. Spittle formed at his lips as though he had been poisoned. Isha cast a shield to block the demon's influence, but he could do nothing to reverse it. Without Chala, Davos would die a slow and painful death.

The youth they called Banchic was not one of his people. He regretted saying it out loud. When the guards tried to seize the young man, Saida's staff knocked them to the ground. She stood between the guards and the man.

Chala had trained her well. Too well.

"Stop this at once. He has been adopted into my herd," Isha said. The asura guards picked themselves up, laughing dangerously while drawing their crooked swords.

"Retribution," they said in unison. One dared to lick its lips. The other glared at Saida, mouthing insults.

"This woman is of my herd. Stand back," Isha commanded.

"No mortal may raise a weapon against a guard of the King," the one said. "Retribution is our right."

"She barely grazed you," he said. "Leave her be. Find the cat."

"There was no cat, Lord Isha. It is a fool's errand," the one replied.

"Insolence! Do you forget who I am?" He was relieved when they put away their weapons and relented. "Carry this man and follow us. Take your claim of retribution to your captain. For now, my herdwoman comes with me." Isha rose to his full height. He would let the bureaucracy handle the complaint if the guards were foolish enough to admit to their captains that they had been bested by a mortal woman.

Isha's chambers had never been so full. Davos lay on a pallet that had been brought by palace servants eager to supply Isha's demands. While Oumo sat despondent in a chair, muttering about how his wagon was irreplaceable, Saida and Banchic stared at Isha.

"You're changed, Lord Isha," Saida said, "How are you?"

"I don't know what you mean," he replied.

*She can see that I am under Hiranyakshipu's influence. I hope they will forgive me.*

Saida had always been Chala's favourite. Isha was surprised that she had decided to remain. Was it out of love for Oumo or the shame of Davos's public rejection?

"Lord Isha, may I ask: how did you know about the cat?" Saida asked.

Isha remembered the fearless young child she had been, a warrior's spirit from birth. She was the brightest of her generation.

*I will not be able to protect her from the King. Yet, she is all I have left of Chala.*

"I keep watch over my herd. There are no cats, and then one appears. At the same time, the herd disappears, and the well of Katora is filled. I am simply curious," he replied.

"Lord Isha," the Katoran youth said, "do you honour the Greater Gods or the Asura King?"

"Must I choose?" Isha asked.

*Will the words freeze in my throat as they did with my Chala?*

"The Asura King goes against all the herd stands for, My Lord," Oumo said from his seat. "Why did you choose to serve him when you could have remained with the herd?"

"I have not found a way to break his hold on me," Isha said, "I am tied to his yoke." There, he had said it aloud.

"My Lord!" Isha did not expect a wave of empathy from Saida. She knelt at his feet. "You must fight and break the yoke, My Lord."

"How, without defeating him?" Isha was aware of a ringing in his ears. How could he tell them their words spoken out loud were not safe? "He is invincible. My only hope is to send you to the safety of the herd and the mortal realm."

"We made our choice to stay," Saida said.

"Why did you stay, Saida?" Isha asked. "You are Chala's favourite." Saida blushed with the praise. "Surely, you do not expect to grow a child now?"

"I will give her a child." The drunken voice belonged to Davos, who had chosen that moment to sit up and groan. "I am the stud; she is my mare. When I call, she comes."

Saida stood frozen, mortified.

Banchic was the first to move. He lifted Davos's face by the hair and landed a fist into the older man's face, knocking him out cold. He waved his hand in pain, gritting his teeth.

Banchic immediately dropped Davos's head and assumed a remorseful stance, his gaze darting to Oumo and Saida as any hot-tempered herd born youth deferring to his elders.

"The blow is on my behalf," Oumo said before Banchic could apologize. "Saida, forgive me. I should have done as much long ago."

"We should have abandoned that one," Isha said. "We are all from one family. That is the first rule of the herd. Chala was right to leave him behind. He broke his promise to you when he asked to come with me."

*Chala was right to leave me behind. I broke my promise when I left the herd.* The realization stung.

The gong sounded a summons for Isha. "Wait here. I must go," he said, embarrassed to have received a summons from the King in front of his people. They were the ones he should be answering. Isha had aimed high but fallen low, no longer the wise protector of his people.

## A Lion's Head

Hiranyakshipu had not missed their arrival. "What is this I hear tell of a cat wandering my halls?" he asked Isha.

"A trifle, My Lord. My herdsman has lost his pet," Isha said. "I worry there are asura who might make a meal out of the creature."

"Tell me: where does the spirit of a mortal go when it is released?" the King asked.

"Is this why you summoned me? I would think one as great as yourself already knew these things."

"I was thinking of how to keep my promise to you, Isha. I want to return your people to their herd," he said. "Wouldn't releasing your mortals to their next life be a start?" His smile drew Isha in.

Isha focused on the King's moustache and sharp fangs. He was under the King's spell, for a long moment, enamoured, enslaved, content in the yoke Hiranyakshipu had him harnessed in.

"Sire, killing is—"

"Wrong? Not if it sends them to the herd." The King toyed with him. "You cannot go, but they can . . . or can you?"

Isha pulled himself away. He would not go against his deepest convictions. He was under the yoke, but his innate stubbornness had no limit.

Out of long habit, he stomped a heel on the stone floor, but there was no comforting earth to ground him.

"Maha Isha Sura, what happens to a cornered bull?" the King asked, circling Isha. Hiranyakshipu had grown in height, or was it that Isha had shrunk?

"Sire, if you have no further need for me, I will attend to my people," Isha replied, pulling away. He would fight the hold the King had on him to the end.

"I am not done with you," the King commanded.

"My Lord," Isha tilted his head, standing his ground.

"Your people will follow my rules. No mortal weapons may kill inside these grounds. No mortals may strike an asura. The punishment will be death." The King spoke in a low tone. "I am told you have among your people a warrior woman who has assaulted one of my asura guards—do you wish for her justice to be meted out by the guard, or should I trust you to handle the matter?"

Isha was speechless.

## A Lion's Head

"Let us make an experiment: show me this woman," the King commanded.

Isha created the vision in mid-air. He was weak, and the vision appeared as a haze. Davos was losing to the demon. Isha would not be able to use him much longer.

*Channa's face came into focus, looking into Davos'ss face as he spoke.*

"What a loyal captain you have there, Isha. Let me gift this vision with sound," the King said.

"He is demon-touched. How will he join our ranks?" Channa asked.

"I want a meaningful life!" Davos exclaimed. His gaze drifted to Oumo and Saida sitting together on the couch.

"Why did you marry me, Davos?" Saida asked.

"Honestly?" Davos said. "I was bored. I can't believe how stupid you are, cuckolding Oumo.

"What use are you, old geezer? Can you not perform as a man?"

Saida moved faster than expected. Davos's head hit the wall as her staff impacted his chest. She followed through with the point of her staff at his throat. Channa reacted even quicker, his knife at her throat as a warning.

"I have only ever loved Oumo. I was mistaken to marry you." She glared at Davos.

Channa lowered his knife.

"I dissolve our marriage." Saida lowered her staff.

In one smooth motion, Davos grabbed Channa's knife and threw it. Saida lunged, but it was too late to stop the knife. Oumo collapsed with the knife in his gut.

"Oumo!" Banchic was at his side.

Time slowed to a crawl. The King cackled. The vision shifted as Davos's head fell to the floor. Isha had no doubt he would find Saida's dagger in his left eye.

The haze that was Isha's vision collapsed into a thousand droplets falling to the floor as rain. Davos was dead.

"Well, that's all the evidence I need," the King said.

Isha's hearing was filled with intense ringing. His fear caused him to see red.


He staggered to get to his quarters after the King had swept out of the audience chamber, too late to save Oumo. Channa would have already taken Saida and the Katoran to safety.

No evidence remained of their having been there.

The elder still clung to life, his slow wheeze alternating with shudders of intense pain.

*The poor fool fought for life!*

Isha pulled Oumo into his arms, overcome with regret. Tears streamed down his cheeks.

"Lord Isha, have I done you wrong?" Oumo said, his voice raspy.

"No, Oumo. I am the one who wronged all of you." Isha would not bring him back, not into a world ruled by Hiranyakshipu. "Where does it hurt?"

"I go to My Lady. She calls me to the light." The elder's gaze was transfixed on something far away. "I will roam."

"Oumo, where is she? Tell me where she is!" Isha pleaded, dropping his facade. "Please, Oumo, tell her that I love her. Tell her I miss her. Tell her I will always regret not staying with the herd."

"Lord Isha, I will be a hunter in the next life." Oumo's lips were tinged blue. "I will see my Sinha again. You . . . you . . ." Oumo turned his wide-eyed gaze on Isha's face in fear. His eyes closed, his face shook, then he died.

"Oumo!" Isha's loneliness enveloped him in its cocoon. Oumo was gone. His faith had been greater than that of all those who remained standing. A sudden weakness overcame Isha as he embraced Oumo's body. The ringing in his ears grew louder, reaching a crescendo before vanishing.

Davos and Oumo's spirits were still trapped within their corporal bodies.

"Oumo is dead. May his spirit be drawn to our people," Isha intoned. He could not accompany Oumo's spirit as Chala would have. He could not see where it went. To the empty room, he said, "Think of him and remember his life. Your memories will draw him. He will go home. May you return to the herd, Oumo.

"Davos is dead. May his spirit walk free," Isha intoned, casting the spell. The two bodies turned to ash. He heard a wail and saw the formless shadow of the demon that had attached itself to Davos in this life. With no advance preparation to entrap it, he watched it evaporate—it would seek out Davos in his next life.

---

"We've got to move fast," Channa said, "Saida, they will come for you."

"But, Oumo . . . We left Oumo." She spoke through her tears. "He will die alone."

"You'll be dead if you stay here; Come on!"

Channa dragged Banchic and Saida down a passage. Still at her wits' end, he acted. He had collected Saida's weapon from Davos's corpse, cleaned it on his tunic, and pressed it into her numb hands.

They arrived at his rooms. Saida had enough time to make out the small rugs and decor, personalizing the space. There were seven cots.

"Quick, get changed," he said. "We need to convince them you've died."

Before she could react, Saida felt him grab her hair, felt the wind of his passing blade. In one quick motion, he had sliced off the length of it. She and Banchic exchanged their clothing for that of the palace guard.

"Follow me," Channa said.

She did her best, head tilted, gaze downward, intent on following him. He took them through the palace gardens. The winding path led around the exterior of the palace complex. Rounding a small set of rooms, they followed Channa up the steps until they reached their destination.

Channa opened the massive, engraved wooden door. Inside the room were two princes. The one dressed in blue sat cross-legged on a bench, deep in a trance. Another prince, younger than the first, dressed in crimson robes with a white cherry blossom motif, met them at the door.

"Please, Lord Bashkala, Lord Prahlada, we need your help," Channa began.

"I'm afraid you're too late," Bashkala said, the regret visible on his downturned face.

Saida backed down the steps, pulling along a confused Banchic. Behind Prince Bashkala, she could see the blue Prince transform into a tall, heavy-set asura with flowing black hair, a black moustache, and golden robes: the Asura King.

They left Channa transfixed, mesmerized by the King's charisma. She was goddess-blessed. She had control of herself. "Run!" she screamed.

Banchic pulled her wrist as they bolted down the empty hallway. Without a map or a guide, they would be lost.

Hiranyakshipu's laughter followed their footfalls. Though the Greater Gods were on their side, she and Banchic were only mortal.

# A Lion's Head

---

*Without my people in this realm, who will I be? What will I become?*

Isha had lived for several millennia in service to the herd. His life and energy depended on his people. The truth that he had been pushing them away all this time burned in his mind.

*They are better off without me.*

He had the power to send his people to the herd. He had to find Channa and Saida.

*I must protect and serve my people.*

The gong sounded; he was being summoned. Compulsion stopped him in his tracks—he had to serve his King. A fluttering of hope gave him strength. Perhaps through death, he could send his people home, liberating them from the madness of Hiranyakshipu's rule.

When Bashkala met him at the door to the audience chamber, the Prince's sombre mood interrupted his black thoughts. Was he a bull being led to the slaughter? Had he played into Hiranyakshipu's plan?

Two guards stood before the King, the same two Saida had assaulted. Isha wanted to crush their smug faces as he braced himself for whatever the King had in store.

"Bested by a woman." Hiranyakshipu was in a good mood. "I will have you both whipped to within an inch of your lives, and then you might be allowed to work in the stables."

The guards were dismissed. Only Bashkala remained for his audience with the King.

"She was captured?" Hiranyakshipu asked.

"Her spirit was released with fire, Father," Prince Bashkala said.

Saida was dead?

"Lord Isha, you were holding out on me with your warriors," the King said. "She took down no less than three of my asura."

Feeling dizzy, Isha leaned against a nearby pillar. He blinked his unseeing eyes and shook his head to suspend his disbelief. "She was of my herd. You had no right." She was Chala's favourite. How could she be gone?

Bashkala approached him with Saida's long braid coiled in his fist. "This is all that remains of her, Maha Isha Sura. I am so sorry."

He looked at the length of thick hair offered. She had been all that remained of his Chala.

## A Lion's Head

"May I?" Isha picked up the length of Saida's hair.

Touching it brought the vision of Saida overwhelmed by a squadron of seven asura. After killing three, she blinded one, incapacitated two, and inflicted injury to the rest before succumbing to her fate.

Another of his people had returned to the herd. He smiled, feeling joy for the first time in weeks. He shook his head. *I should be sad, yet I am relieved.*

"I believe we see as one, together," the King said, "You should honour her strength, Maha Isha Sura."

"Yes, My Lord," Isha replied. He was compelled to keep the braid. He would honour her by placing it around his neck.

*This is no honour!* The deepest part of his mind screamed.

Hiranyakshipu looked pleased." Come, brother," he said, "let us dine."

# 13

By mid-morning, Sinha had found the kitchen. He feigned a nap, curled up with his tail tucked under his head at the hearth. Marking his appearance, the head cook had done nothing to chase him away.

"Cook, did he try poison?" asked a young pot boy as he filled a pot with water.

"Yes, I was ordered—ME—to put poison in the Prince's food. I would not!" Olu was a rotund lady with grey hair in a bun held in place by a skewer. She bore a vague resemblance to Oumo. Sinha had determined she was adept at managing the kitchen despite her appearance. She wore an ill-fitting, mismatched red skirt and pink blouse with wooden buttons puckered at her chest. Her attention was on the pot of bubbling stew.

"What happened then?" A kitchen maid broke long beans and sorted the edible seeds into one basket and the waste into another.

"They sent me home for a few weeks. All I know is the Prince was still alive when I came back, praise the Lord." The last three words were said in a whisper. Olu threw mustard seeds and onions into the hot oil to sizzle.

## A Lion's Head

"Some *father*—ordering the guards to beat his son soon after. They refused." Olu's assistant was a tall woman with a low voice. Her well-oiled hair was pulled tight in a neat bun. Her spice-stained clothing hung loose on her lanky form. She deftly ground pepper, garlic, and onions between two stones. She had unconsciously marked her forehead with rice flour.

"I remember that herd of parade elephants that went on a rampage through the city, and the Prince just stood there." The girl finished with her beans and took the boy's place at the spout. She washed them before carefully dispensing them in the boy's pot.

"Yes! The elephants ran past him like he wasn't even there. Destroyed the whole street *and* the market!" The assistant cleared the yellow paste she had made into several ornate wooden serving dishes and wiped down the stones with water and cloth.

"Aye, it took them two seasons to rebuild," Olu added.

"I heard the Prince was found in the snake pit," the younger girl said, dispensing a variety of powdered and whole spices into her pot.

"I dunno, but, for sure, it had to be yon father's doing. The snake keeper was shocked to open the door in the morning, meaning to throw in some'un, only to find the snakes in a pile and yon Prince asleep! Not a scratch on him!" answered the Olu's assistant.

"It's a miracle."

"He's the miracle," the pot boy said.

"Did you know he fell in the river and nearly drowned?"

"I'd say he was pushed."

"Lady Bhudevi saw him and had her man pull him out," said Olu, sounding tired. Her eyes watered as she chopped onions. "She was sent to live in the country soon after that. Probably to avoid his Lord Almighty." She rolled her eyes and, a moment later, tightened her jaw with anger. "The last straw was her ladyship, Holika, taking the Prince's place on the pyre."

"May she be blessed in the next life," the others said in unison, each of them touching their palms together. The silence was marred by the pop of burning wood and the sizzle of frying onions.

"Guard coming!" shrieked the girl, who had briefly left the small room and returned with a string of garlic.

"It's all right, it's just yon Olu's son, the captain," Olu's assistant confirmed.

Olu had put herself between the door and Sinha. She gave him a measured glance before her son arrived.

"Omma!" A nervously, energetic, dark-haired man in a deep purple uniform entered the room. His handsome, chiselled, tanned features drew a fluttering of eyelashes and blushes from the younger servants. He rubbed a hand down his face and scratched his thick mutton chop sideburns.

"My Channa—what brings you here?" Olu gritted her teeth and waved off her three helpers. She pulled him by the elbow out of the kitchen and into a private alcove.

Sinha rose and followed and sat at their heels.

"Omma, I don't know how to put this: Davos, Oumo, and Saida are—"

"Dead. Do you forget I have the second sight? Oumo came to me in my dreams. You think my brother would leave without saying goodbye?" Olu wiped away a tear, "We've no time to mourn." Her voice broke with the last words. She patted her eyes and face with a moist towel hanging from her hip. "He gave me a message: the well is dry; a hero is nearby." She raised herself to kiss her tall son on the cheek.

"Omma, I feel so helpless. I tried . . ." Channa held his mother against his chest, choking back tears.

"You are of the herd, my son. You do, in good faith, what any of us would do. Lord Isha should have heeded our Goddess. Now, he calls the Asura King 'master'." She patted his back. "I have something for you." She raised her voice to speak loudly, startling her helpers as they sought to eavesdrop. "There is a filthy cat in here. Disgusting! Please remove it."

Her dutiful son swooped in and grabbed Sinha by the scruff of his neck. Sinha was too surprised to register any hurt. He let his body go limp.

"I told Oumo I would help in any way I could. The cat-lion must get to the Prince," she whispered.

"I will do what I can." Channa carried Sinha clumsily out of the kitchen and to the gardens shaded by frangipani trees. "What use has His Grace for a cat?"

Nevertheless, he carried Sinha through a maze of halls and outer buildings. The farther from the kitchen, the quieter the palace grounds became.

He was crossing through a covered walkway bracketed by pleasure gardens when a familiar voice spoke from behind. "Channa, I have been looking for you."

Channa kept walking.

"Is that Oumo's cat?"

Channa feigned tripping and drop-threw Sinha, who deftly landed and dashed to the left into the dense foliage of the nearest pleasure garden.

"Is that Oumo's cat? Did you let it escape?" Isha's black embroidered robes swept the ground as he walked.

"My Lord, you said you were looking for me," Channa said, but his gaze challenged the bull-headed god. "What has the Asura King done to you, Lord Isha, that you no longer protect the herd?"

"Tell me what happened to Chala's favourite, Saida—wasn't she with you?"

"It was as if the King had planned everything," Channa said.

"No, that can't be true." Isha drew himself to his full height.

"Lord, you no longer protect us." Channa fearfully backed away from the bull-headed god.

"How could Saida die?" Isha picked him up and shook him like a rag doll. "What happened?"

"Where were you?" Channa shouted back in anger. "Why did you take us from our herd?
"

"I did not abandon the herd," Isha bellowed, his eyes red and full of tears.

"Is that Saida's hair?" Barely visible around Isha's neck was a familiar coil of braided human hair. Channa grasped the necklace from around his god's neck and pulled. It would not budge. "Lord, we do not desecrate the dead. Take the braid off!"

The fury of Isha's fists hit Channa. He flew through the air. His body crumpled against a stone post.

"Isha Sura, *you* are the one abandoned by the herd." Channa gasped, his stamina and words fuelled by righteous anger. "The goddess left you. You are not yourself. May Lady Chala protect me." Channa curled in a fetal position, protecting his head from Isha's blows.

"She did not leave me!" the asura bellowed.

## A Lion's Head

Sinha watched helplessly from his vantage point up a tree. There was something wrong with the Water Buffalo Asura.

"If you were a part of the herd, you would know where they went." Channa moaned as Isha Sura trampled him. He said nothing more.

"You lie. I will send you to the h—" Isha froze, realizing his violent actions. His hands shook. His ears fell. He blinked vacant eyes.

"What have I done? Channa, my eyes, my sight—where have the colours gone?" He backed away from Channa's fallen form. "Forgive me!

"What am I doing? What is happening to me? None of you are safe." He turned and fled.

Sinha waited.

Channa lay unresponsive.

He retrieved the bottle of holy water and returned with it to Channa's prone body as darkness fell. The bottle was stoppered and could not be opened without hands. Sinha yowled in frustration.

Four guards approached. "Ahoy, there! Who is it that cries?"

Sinha hid.

"Who would bring a child to the palace?" one asked.

"I swear I heard a baby cry," said the second, his eyes darting to the dark corners of the dark, silent gardens.

"Channa! Fool! I told him not to roam alone, but he insisted on seeing his mother." The third motioned with his hands for the first two to watch for trouble.

"I should have gone with him!" The fourth fell to Channa's side. "He's not responding!"

"Let's take him to His Grace. He'll know what to do," the third said.

The men picked up their fallen comrade. Sinha followed quietly in their wake. In hushed voices, they spoke of their hatred of the asura palace. The guards were armed with curved swords that hung from their belts. Like Channa, their oiled hair was tied in a utilitarian top knot without ornamentation. Several more passages leading to palace buildings followed. Finally, they paused in a long, empty hallway. This section of the palace was built of wood. Intricate panel carvings of the King and his exploits allowed nothing but a cool breeze to pass through. The floor was of polished wood. The rooms were all located to the right. They carried Channa to the first empty room.

"Prince Prahlada," said one of the guards in hushed tones to the Prince standing in the hallway. "We found Channa in a bad state."

The Prince's features were too perfect to be human. He was a younger version of Hiranyakshipu, his features softer with youth or a gift from his mother. As an asura, he stood a head taller than the men. He wore a simple tunic and pants of light blue linen covered in a dense embroidery of silver and blue swirls and lotus motifs. His oiled black hair had been styled as a braided top knot. A turtleshell comb carved with a lotus motif adorned the knot. As he moved, Sinha smelled traces of patchouli diffusing into the air.

The prince swept into the room.

"He bears traces of my father's magic." The Prince placed his hands on Channa's temples. A few moments passed in silence except for the shuffle of impatient feet and the nervous cough of one of the men.

"He is concussed," Prahlada said. "Men, I am sorry: he is dying."

Sinha had gone unnoticed until this moment. He meowed.

The guards reacted as one. Each had their hands on their swords but did not draw.

Prahlada's hand rose, palm out, to set them at ease.

"You came," he said to the cat.

Sinha padded up to the prince and dropped the stoppered bottle in his lap. *Healing water, Prince Prahlada.*

"Your arrival is well-timed." Prahlada unstoppered the bottle and dispensed a drop to Channa's lips. The bottle vanished into one of the folds of the Prince's sleeves. "Now, we wait. May the Gods protect him."

Addressing the guards, he said, "Stay with Channa."

"You, accompany me," he said to Sinha. The Prince rose from his position at Channa's head and led the way out the door.

Sinha followed the Prince down the empty hall. They passed a second room containing scrolls, writing implements, sealed boxes, and what looked to be the Prince's sleeping quarters. They entered the third and smallest room, where the Prince sat down cross-legged. Unlike the other rooms, the windows in this room were draped with decorative reed woven mats, allowing for light to pass through and a modicum of privacy from the outside world. The lotus-scented room was warm.

## A Lion's Head

"I dreamed you would arrive," Prahlada said. "I trust the Gods sent you to help me."

*You with your father—where do you stand?*

"My faith conflicts with my father's ambitions," the Prince replied. "Until I relent, I am confined to my rooms. I pray he will realize that his actions and beliefs are wrong." Tears fell from Prahlada's downcast eyes. "He may have wrong views, but he is still my father."

*You will be here a long time.* Sinha said.

"Yes, he will not relent," Prahlada said. "We are at a stalemate."

Though uncomfortable, the transformation did not hurt. Sinha felt hot. He shook himself, but his body burned. The fragrance of lotus, tulsi, and patchouli blended, captivating his senses. Tawny fur flowed upward and outward, covering his groin and legs to give the impression of clothing. The ginger hairs on his head grew longer and denser to reveal a mane of thick red hair. He grew taller until he was looking down at the Prince, his body transforming into that of a muscular, copper-skinned youth. His hands and feet ended in dagger-like, razor-sharp claws. His tail whipped behind him. He saw his face reflected in Prahlada's eyes: he wore the head of a lion.

He was a hybrid: a man-lion—the only one of his kind. He bowed low with feline grace as the Prince stood.

"Your Highness," Sinha bowed again, politely allowing Prahlada to cover his surprise. Sinha's new eyes saw what his feline eyes could not: Prahlada was covered from head to toe in bruises at various stages of healing. The Prince held himself stiffly.

*Prahlada, Adult though he may be, is a battered child. He doesn't know from where the next blow will fall.*

"Did those hurt?" he asked.

"What?" replied the Prince.

"It seems to me you need the holy water yourself," Sinha persisted.

"Oh, you mean my appearance." The Prince shuffled his feet and looked down. "I respect my father," the Prince replied. "He is king." The two stood in awkward silence.

"Lord Prahlada, please, take of the holy water." He waited while the prince took the stopper out of the small bottle and took a drop. The bruises faded. The Prince's posture shifted as tendons and bone realigned.

"Thank you for coming, *Narasinha*. I have had the same dream for a fortnight: the gods sent you to help me. Are you here to warn me of the next challenge my father will set?" the Prince asked.

"I am what the gods sent," Sinha replied. He presented his clawed hands in a flourish, and bowed to the Prince for a third time. "Be ready for what comes next."

With a sense of foreboding, his body cooled as he transformed back into his cat form. This would be his last time as a cat. He stretched and ran from the room before the Prince could ask what he planned to do.

*Prahlada is a child who believes his father will come around.*

Sinha's paws made no sound and left no trace on the palace's polished marble floors. He skidded to a stop, sliding into a pillar with a soft thump and casually walked into the gardens. By moonlight, he contemplated the situation: the King will kill his son in his quest to reign supreme. He considered his options.

# 14

As day turned to dusk, Sinha found a means to climb up to the beams holding the roof over the palace. From this vantage point, he could observe undetected. He sneezed as the dust from countless incense burners gathered in the warm air beneath the rafters. A fire-bringing spell carried on a soft, gentle breeze, which illuminated the dozens of bronze lamps below. Sinha remained invisible to the asura gathered below him, most of whom were low-ranking, no more than demons.

Hiranyakshipu summoned his eldest son. Several asura blew on conch shells while others played flute and drum.

The bull-headed god stood by the King. Was it a trick of the eye, or had he shrunk? He held back his urge to hiss. Whipping his tail set off a plume of dust. His sneeze went unnoticed under the musical interlude preceding the Prince's entrance.

Maha Isha Sura was visibly startled when Channa entered. Head held high, he was unmistakable due to his exaggerated sideburns. The Prince and his men followed. Channa kept his gaze forward, ignoring the presence

## A Lion's Head

of his bull-headed god. His men moved slowly in time to the beat of a drum.

Isha Sura's eyes seemed to bore into Channa as they approached, and his ears flicked.

The Prince's serene demeanour was in sharp contrast to the scowl of irritation his father wore. Prahlada was dressed in a simple tunic and light blue linen pants. He wore a simple unadorned silver circlet on his forehead.

"Greetings, Father, you look well." The Prince bowed in obeisance to his father. The King was dressed in heavily embroidered gold and black robes, his hair loose, falling in great waves down his back. He wore a tall, ornately gilded crown with the horns of a bull.

He rose from his dais, carrying his heavy mace of office, made from steel and embossed with silver and gold. As if testing the Prince's resolve, the King tapped his son on the shoulder and knee with his mace.

Prince Prhalada did not lose his composure, though he did straighten his back and loosen his muscles in anticipation of a strike.

"Have you heard, my son? Ishwara's well has run dry," said the King.

Though Prahlada's expression remained neutral, Sinha sensed his hope stir.

The King opened his arms and made a sweeping movement to all assembled. "Do you see an all-mighty hero nearby?"

"The Supreme Lord of the universe is everywhere, sir," Prahlada replied.

"Prahlada, who is the Supreme Lord of the universe, my son?"

"Sir, you know my answer," the Prince said.

"Tell again, son." His father spat as he spoke. A slave appeared to wipe the spittle from the polished marble floor. As usual, a group of Prince Prahlada's followers had gathered under armed guard to watch the spectacle. Some rocked as they sang devotional prayers to safeguard their Prince. The guards beat back any who voiced outrage or slogans of confidence in his support.

Prahlada sighed.

"The Supreme Lord is not you, sir."

"Who else but *me*, a supreme being who is above everything, someone who can control everyone and is all-pervading?" He struck the back of Prahlada's thighs with the mace, throwing the Prince forward and onto his knees.

## A Lion's Head

The Prince hissed in pain, quickly regaining his calm, his arms outstretched and fingers touching the cool marble floor as he faced the floor. "Yes, sir."

"Where is *he*, Prahlada? If *he* is everywhere, why is *he* not present before me?" The King's eyes were enlarged, and his mouth twisted with rage.

"He is here, sir. He is on the ground. He is in the air. He is in the dust," Prhalada answered.

The king spat upon the ground. Once more, the slave moved to wipe it up. "*Leave* it." He drop-kicked the slave with one fluid motion.

He pointed to the ornately carved wooden pillar on which Sinha was perched with his mace. "So you're telling me he's in this pillar? "

"Yes, sir."

Hiranyakshipu's rage sent the mace through the pillar. It smashed, and with it came down a portion of the stone roof. Shale tiles exploded from the force of impact. The marble floor was covered in shrapnel and dust. The blue sky at dusk presented itself overhead.

Sinha dropped from the sky, transforming into his half-human, half-lion form. An overwhelming sense of righteous anger and rage overcame him.

*What is this rage?*

He gave in to the feeling and roared a blood-curdling sound. Before anyone could react, he'd snatched up the startled Hiranyakshipu in his skin-piercing claws. Sinha landed on the floor with one knee bent and the other to the floor. Dropping the King on his raised knee, he felt satisfied by the feel and sound of the crack of the King's back upon impact.

"Neither day nor night. Neither inside nor outside. Neither in the air nor touching the earth." Sinha spoke in a deep, sonorous voice as he pierced the dying Hiranyakshipu's flesh with his claws, felt his heart burst within his broken chest cavity. "My claws are neither weapon, palm, nor fist. I am neither human, deity, demon, nor animal!"

The world moved in slow motion. The guards loyal to the Prince remained while the others dropped weapons and fled, spreading word of the King's death in their wake.

"Father!" The Prince fell to his knees. Individuals loyal to the Prince stepped forward.

"It had to be done," Sinha growled, consumed by righteous anger. His claws contracted, and he gently placed the broken body of the dead King on the ground.

"Leave me," *King* Prahlada commanded. Divine light shone through the hole in the roof, lighting up the new King from above. His five brothers approached with caution to kneel before him.


More of King Prahlada's people gathered. A peacock fluted, signalling the arrival of Lord Sakka, Lord Indra, Lady Prajapati, and the pantheon of Greater Gods.

This was no place for Sinha's righteous anger. He roared his welcome to the Gods as they manifested. Then, he leaped past the remaining guards, measuring their loyalty to King Prahlada as he passed. His job was not finished. His anger was not sated.

He stalked through the palace compound. The demons he encountered turned to black smoke upon impact with his claws. He sought one asura in particular. "*Maha Isha Sura*, where are you?" he called. "I am Sinha, and I have been watching you."

The bellow of a water buffalo sounded as he stood at the palace gates. It was all the warning he received before the bull's head and horns impacted his side, sending Sinha into a shed. "You? Oumo's cat?"

Sinha was up in a second and on his prey, claws unleashed, a snarl escaping from his throat. He landed on the bull-headed god with his hands and feet extended for maximum damage. Sinha's rage did not dispel, though he left his foe battered, bleeding, and bruised.

Adrenaline and righteous anger fuelled his legs as he ran through the city. He spotted the dark shadows of fleeing demons and sprang for what passed as its throat.

He rounded the gates, catching the two gargoyle demons unawares.

More demons and asura fled to escape his wrath. Sinha chased the guilty out of the city. Word of his actions spread like wildfire: "Hiranyakshipu is dead. His killer, a man-lion, is on the rampage."

Sinha stopped to free people who had been enslaved. Their guards dropped their weapons and fled at the sight of him.

His senses were magnified in his man-lion form. Sinha sought out every last captive within the city and liberated them. He kept his promise to the God Ishwara not to harm a single human.

## A Lion's Head

The last batch of slaves had been at a tannery. He had turned a corner in a poor district of the capital, when a familiar voice called out to him in the darkness. There were no lamps. The stench of urine was incredible.

"Is that you, cat?"

"Banchic?" Sinha's anger evaporated when he heard the young man's voice.

Banchic came forward limping.

"Are you hurt?"

"Did you succeed?" Banchic asked.

"I did. Hiranyakshipu is no more. King Prahlada sits on the throne." Sinha replied.

Banchic collapsed at his feet. "Good. Sir Sinha, please, can you take me home?"

Sinha picked up the young man. Banchic's pulse was weak.

Not knowing what to do other than to turn his senses to find Oumo and Saida. Sinha tried to picture the old man but saw a butterfly fighting a breeze instead. He looked for Saida and failed. Then, he remembered: the cook's words. They were dead.

Sinha's battle rage spent, he carried Banchic to the river. His muscles burned from overuse. He stretched and arched his back. He flexed his body to bring about relaxation and clear the anger and violence from his flesh.

He stood on the flats of his feet, hips overhead, looking down at his outstretched hands, and saw for the first time his blood-soaked arms and body.

He washed himself in the river using sand to scrub the indeterminant matter from his claws. The water was cold, but he persisted until it ran clear.

Sinha suddenly felt overcome with exhaustion. He sat cross-legged in lotus pose to rest, his mind was quiet as he sat and observed, focusing only on the moment and his breath. Banchic lay forgotten by his side as the sun began to rise on the horizon.

"Lord Man-Lion, *Narasinha?*" The voice was of an older man. "We wish to give you our thanks."

Sinha cracked an eye and was startled to see a crowd had gathered. Three mortal women attended to Banchic. Several more laid a feast before him. Sinha's gaze met the speaker's, an ancient man bent with age.

"Our people will never forget your service," the man said.

"Thank you," Sinha said. The people nearest him backed away at the sound of his rough, deep voice. Others pointed and spoke in awestruck, hushed tones. They were afraid of him.

"No, My Lord, *we* thank *you*!" Old as he was, the man shakily dropped to his knees.

"No, no, please. You don't need to." Sinha stood and drew the old man back up. Sinha felt shame when the elder cried out and several people in the crowd backed away. He did not know how to retract his over-long claws.

The senior pressed his palms together and bowed from the hip. The mob was on its knees, worshipping him again.

*What do I do?*

He ate the food they offered, and the ladies pressed him to eat more. The food was delicious, a far cry from the humble gruel he had shared with Oumo. He had to hold his hand over his plate to get them to stop serving him. All the while, he kept asking for news of Banchic.

Finally, an older woman approached. "I'm sorry. There's little we can do," she said. "He is too weak."

Sinha remembered the holy water. His first thought was to take Banchic to his village. He thanked everyone for their help and the food, but as he tried to move, a new crowd blocked him, wanting to give their thanks.

"Please, I just need to get him to help," he pleaded. He had to dissuade their "helpful" offers of assistance.

Frustrated, he exclaimed, "I must get back to the palace! King Prahlada needs me. Stand aside!"

The crowd parted.

Sinha carried Banchic to the crowded palace grounds, bypassing the long queue of officials waiting to pledge allegiance to the young king. He carried Banchic, wondering how he would gain access to Prahlada.

Prahlada's guards held their spears crossed, blocking his entry. Sinha recognized Channa. "Channa, let me speak to the King!"

"The Man-Lion . . . Men, let him through," Channa said. He led Sinha into the audience chamber. "I recognize this man you carry, but how do you know me?"

Sinha explained how he had been Oumo's cat and how he had discovered Banchic.

"Follow me." Channa led Sinha to the front of the queue. "Lord *Narasinha* is here, Your Majesty," he announced.

Sinha again explained his situation. "King Prahlada, can you revive him?" he asked.

## A Lion's Head

"If this is what you wish, Narasinha. Channa took hours to revive." The King accompanied them to an empty room.

Each of the room's porous walls depicted an elaborate mandala. The openings to the gardens allowed for a sweet-smelling breeze. Since the King's ascension, flowers bloomed, and the boughs of trees hung heavy with fruit. The pitter-patter of rain drummed steadily on the roof.

"The Gods informed me that you were the key to my father's riddle," Prahlada said, giving Sinha a long, measuring look.

"I was," Sinha replied. "Can you forgive me for taking his life?"

"I have already done so," the King said. "I accept why the Gods made you—what will you do now?"

"I don't know," Sinha said. "I have not thought about it."

"May I rely on your aid to rid these lands of demons and malicious asura?" Prahlada asked. He explained his plan to restore the immortal lands: the humans would be sent back to the mortal realm with any asura wishing to accompany them, while the demons would be banished to the netherworlds. There would be many battles ahead.

Though Prahlada was king, he still had to conquer his father's remaining loyalists, including Maha Isha Sura.

"I wish to make peace with the asura. With Father's great power, he set curses that will take a thousand years to undo."

Sinha agreed to help as he could.

Contented and without fanfare, the King left.

Sinha anxiously monitored Banchic's shallow breathing. Eventually, Banchic let out a snore from the cot, and Sinha was finally able to relax while the man slept.

"I do not know what happened to Oumo or Saida," Sinha said, noticing for the first time that Channa was with him. The man sat with his back against the wall, one leg extended and one bent. His bent knee carried the weight of both his elbow and head. Sinha had never seen anyone look so defeated.

As if sensing Sinha's attention, Channa's voice choked on a sob. "Oumo was my maternal uncle. Saida was his wife. She was a formidable woman. Davos was my best friend and cousin. Seeing you, I was reminded of them. I was not there for them. I could not save them."

"It is permissible to grieve, Channa," Sinha said gently, "What happened to them?"

"I don't know if I am ready to put their tragedy into words, My Lord," Channa said.

"I am not your Lord—call me Sinha.

"Perhaps you will speak with me when these events are no longer fresh in your heart," Sinha said. He had never experienced grief before. He was sad to have lost Oumo. He had expected the old man to be there when he'd completed his quest. He felt incomplete in their absence.

Sinha had found the jasmine garden empty. He lay on his back, marvelling at the rain.

"You are soaked, Sinha, sir," Channa said when he found Sinha later. He stood in awkward silence for a long moment before saying, "Some are awed in the presence of their Gods."

"He didn't use to be," Sinha said, remembering Banchic's cheeky encounter with Lord Sakka back in Katora. Banchic's unspoken experience in captivity and his near-death experience had changed him.

After Banchic had recovered, he would not speak of the events leading up to his capture. Instead, he would stare wide-eyed and slack-jawed at Sinha until Channa had taken the initiative to lead him away.

"You are not awed by me?" Sinha asked, turning his head.

Channa seemed to have recovered from his grief. "My people are used to having our Gods among us. While I have great respect for you, I am not intimidated." He shrugged. "For one, you're not my God, but more importantly, I'm not convinced you *are* a God."

His admission brought a laugh to Sinha's lips. "Is it wrong to be soaked by the rain, Herdsman Channa?" he asked, to change the subject.

"It depends. Will you fall sick?" The question sparked a philosophical discussion about whether an asura could get sick, concluding with Channa explaining the conditions that affected human health. With the understanding that humans could catch a chill from the rain, Sinha suggested they continue their conversation indoors. He joined his new friend for dinner that night.

Sinha spent his days watching Banchic from a distance until Prahlada requested the young man return to Katora to prepare his people for their return to the mortal realm. At his departure, Sinha reached out to hug him with unconstrained affection. To his dismay, Banchic recoiled.

"My Lord, Narasinha!" Banchic prostrated himself, worshipping at Sinha's feet. "I am not worthy of all you have done for me. Thank you for saving my life."

Sinha missed being a cat. As the days passed, he missed being able to pass unnoticed.

The asura of Prahlada's court had seen his angry rampage. Fearing a resurgence, they walked on eggshells around him. He wanted to disappear. He did not know where he fit with the courtiers and tradespeople, the new king's brothers, and the other asura. Not wanting to bother Prahlada, Sinha would prowl the gardens at night and keep to the quieter parts of the palace by day.

"Sinha, come join me!" Channa's voice called from above.

He opened tired eyes following a long, gruelling night spent alone with his memories.

Channa stood on an upper balcony. He motioned that Sinha should join him, pointing to an entrance leading to a wooden stairwell.

"Would you accompany me to Lord Isha's rooms?"

Sinha nodded, reluctant to speak. He had not spoken to another being since Banchic had left.

They entered a set of rooms with few pieces of furniture, making it look empty and lonely. The walls had been painted a muddy shade of grey. He followed Channa to the innermost room. There stood the only pleasant item: a moss-green wall installed against one wall.

"I don't know what I expected," Channa said. "I hoped for a message or something."

"You don't see the words?" Sinha asked. He traced the pattern in the wall with a claw:

*Find strength. Gather together.*
*The hero's time has come.*
*The green moss is the cure.*
*When the act is done.*

Channa stood staring at Sinha for a long moment. "Sinha, you are brilliant. The cure ... The cure—how is it the cure? Will it break *his* madness?" He pulled his knife, scraped the wall, and collected the moss as it came away.

"Who suffers from madness?" Sinha asked.

"My Lord Isha Sura," Channa replied.

# 15

**SIX YEARS LATER**

*My body healed. I am alive. I must get out. I will go mad if I stay here.*

Desperation fuelled Sinha's strength. He grunted with the effort needed to push through the rubble. He burrowed upward, finding moist soil and crawled around the rock debris. A wave of relief washed over him when he broke through, his claws touching nothing but air. Relief was replaced by the pain of the sunlight blinding him as he pulled himself out of the ground. Was it worth that much trouble to stay alive?

He itched where the dirt had dried—fusing with his fur—as though he was made of stiff clay. The twisted mound, the result of the landslide, rose above him. He was on the dry side. There had to be water where the river had been. He needed to be free of the mud.

He heard a bellow.

"So, you survived," a dry voice said. "Abomination, what, may I ask, are you called?"

Sinha attempted to speak, but for a long moment, he could do nothing but cough and gag. Finally, dropping to his hands and knees, he threw up. He wiped his mouth with a fist and looked up at the speaker. "Sinha. I'm called Sinha." Sinha's vision was still adjusting to the light, which framed a silhouette, tall, wide, and horned.

"You look pathetic," the voice said with contempt. "I suppose I can't say, 'Look what the cat dragged in.' If you have nine lives, how many do you suppose are left?"

"Enough." Sinha climbed to the top of a rise. There, water pooled, laden with silt. He waded into the cold water, shaking and twisting to release the caked mud from his fur. He'd finished scrubbing himself clean when his nose picked up Channa's scent: well-worn leather and sweat.

He turned to find something unexpected: the bull-headed . . . creature kneeling on the ground, cradling Channa in his arms. His body shook as he wept, moaning a wretched wail of despair. His immaculate black robes were in marked contrast to the red-brown wasteland around him. For the first time, Sinha pitied the fallen god.

"Did you have to kill him?" Sinha asked. His depleted heart had yet to absorb the loss.

"It's your fault." Mahishasura raised his head to reveal bloodshot eyes. "You should not have brought him here." He gently rocked the body.

"I should not have brought him along," Sinha said. "He was a good man. A good friend."

"He was the last," Mahishasura said. "There are no more." He fingered what looked like a length of braided rope around his neck before laying Channa's body on the ground.

Channa looked serene; a stranger would think he slept curled on his side. Sinha had shared the barracks with Channa for long enough to know his friend tossed and kicked in his sleep. He would no longer suffer from nightmares.

Without warning, Channa rose into the air, fire consuming his body. It hung in the air for a split second as a cloud of ash before the wind blew it away.

"He goes back to the herd," Mahishasura said.

"Is that what happened to the others?" Sinha asked. Soon after Hiranyakshipu's death, more than a dozen isolated members of Channa's herd had vanished, one at a time, without a trace. Fearing for their safety, Channa had secured safe passage for his mother, his men, and any remaining herdspeople to settle with Banchic's people, travelling through the stargates to the mortal realm. Channa alone had remained, obsessed with finding his errant god.

"I sent them to the herd," Mahsishasura said with conviction. He stood before Sinha. Sometime between the Asura King's death and that moment, Maha Isha Sura had devolved into a demon. His eyes were bloodshot. His robes hid his diminished form. His horns had shrunken and twisted.

"You're mad," Sinha said, stepping back, suddenly afraid. If Maha Isha Sura had caused the landslide and the waterfall, he was more formidable than any asura Sinha had met in the immortal realm. He held the power to manipulate the fabric of the realm. With a thought, he could send Sinha a hundred horse-lengths underground.

"Are you aware of the price for taking a human life?" Sinha asked. If the demon wanted to bury him, he would have already.

"I have thrice paid the price," Mahishasura said, "The Greater Gods brought us here to suffer. My wife left me. My herd is lost." The demon wailed a long, low keen. "I am alone. Believe me, I paid a price." The ground shook, threatening to break the dam.

"Channa had faith in you." Sinha's anger stirred, supercharging his depleted resources. "He wanted to bring you back to the herd. He did not abandon you! He held the riddle for how you would return to them." Grief came with anger. He blinked wildly, holding back tears, fighting to keep his composure.

"I cannot go back to her." Mahishasura's regret was palpable.

"Who?"

"Chala, my wife. Soon after her favourite, Saida, died, I lost my ability to see colour." Isha stroked the braided necklace of human hair he wore around his neck. "There is no going back for me."

Sinha was speechless.

Saida.

His friend Saida's hair.

He had not found out what had happened to her. Had he killed her?

"I had everything, but my herd vanished the day you appeared. When Chala left me, I lost my connection . . . all that grounded me." Isha's bellow coincided with the dam breaking. The earth beneath their feet churned. "I had nothing left to keep me from my master, Hiranyakshipu—who you murdered. We were one."

Sinha leaped to higher ground, pulling Isha with him. Maybe he could solve this puzzle. Mahishasura operated as if he had two minds. Channa had spoken of Lord Isha as a loving and benevolent god, but as a demon, Mahishasura's perception of events was twisted.

"He was never your master. Channa said you served the herd." Sinha roared. "The King is dead. You are free. Let it go! Free yourself from his bond!" The power unleashed by his righteous anger caused his mane and tail to stand on end.

"No!" The demon bellowed in return.

He could not help himself. He pounded the obstinate buffalo with his fists in frustration. "You fool! You could have gone home!"

"I am not worth saving." Mahishasura moaned. He did not fight back.

Sinha's anger evaporated, replaced by pity. The broken demon clung desperately to Saida's braid.

"Take it off. You have the power to burn it." Sinha said, remembering Channa's insight. "Her hair—it's been cursed."

"I cannot," Isha whispered.

"Your Chala would not want this. Please! Take it off. Burn it. Let her memory go free."

## A Lion's Head

"It's all I have left!" Isha rammed Sinha with his horns, carrying them both into the water. The cold shocked the air from Sinha's lungs. The buffalo held him in a murderous embrace. They were sinking.

Sinha flexed himself free and dragged the demon from the water by his horns. "Obstinate bull: take it off!" he roared.

"No." The buffalo swung his head.

Sinha was thrown back into the water, but he was ready this time. When his feet felt solid ground, he sprang back to the shore. The demon would not escape.

He landed on Mahishasura's back and beat the demon senseless. He would drag him to the palace for judgment. Let the Greater Gods deal with Mahishasura. He was done.

Sinha could not bring himself to touch Saida's cursed hair.

"It has only begun between us," the demon Mahishasura grunted. His horns were broken, and his body was bruised. "I will not forgive you."

Sinha growled in response. He had spent his anger on violence. He was neither proud nor satisfied. King Prahlada had ordered for 'no more deaths.' The asura already called Sinha a ferocious king-slayer. With his capture of Mahishasura, he earned the title, demon-stalker.

Sinha shoved the shackled god-turned-demon toward the stargate keyed to the netherworld. The inky darkness beyond it ate the light. He watched as the demon stepped across the threshold. He was not the only one to shudder and feel relief once the gate had closed.

Hooded naga guards had been stationed at regular intervals in the cave. Torches, fungi, and crystals provided a comforting, warm light to accompany him through the maze and back to daylight. He spoke to no one.

Sinha was no different than the demon he had banished. Mahishasura would be a stranger in the nether realm; Sinha was a stranger to the immortal realm.

*He had lost his herd.*

*I lost my friends.*

Enveloped in a shroud of loneliness, he allowed himself to be escorted out of the underground maze.

Mahishasura's sentencing had been uneventful. He had made many enemies among the asura, and only one of Prahalada's younger brothers, Bashkala, had attended.

## A Lion's Head

The asura had bowed his head to the demon and wished him a future success in returning to his herd. Mahishasura had ignored him.

There had been little time to mourn Channa's death. Sinha claimed his friend's belongings. He had avoided the quarters they'd shared after the herdspeople had left.

Sinha had no need for possessions. He folded Channa's clothes and keepsakes into a blanket. Perhaps he could give them to the naga to repurpose or convey to the mortal realm. Surely, someone would find a use for them.

He fumbled with a small bag left open on the mantle—his claws made it impossible to handle tools built for normal hands.

The bag fell to the ground, about three dozen beads the size of marbles—Channa's most prized possessions—scattered across the floor. The warrior never left his quarters without wearing one on a thong around his neck. He'd given one to each of his people as they parted.

A memory surfaced, causing Sinha to smack his palm against his forehead with gut-wrenching regret. How had he missed it?

At the time, he had not understood why Channa had dried and powdered the moss from the wall.

"He's under a curse," Channa had said. "If not for your reading the moss wall, I would not have found the cure."

Sinha had witnessed the warrior crafting the powder into the precursor for these beads. Channa had polished each marble, hand-painting the outer surface with black lacquer to preserve the moss.

*The green moss will be the cure,* the wall had read.

Sinha did not know if he would ever encounter Mahishasura again. Nevertheless, he asked for help from the palace servants to collect and string the beads on a gold chain he could wear around his neck.

A decade passed before Prahlada's kingdom was secure from demons, and all humans and their descendants had been returned through the stargates to the mortal realm. Sinha would wander the immortal realm, even after King Prahlada outlived his children. After a peaceful reign, one of his grandsons had inherited the kingdom. Their descendants lived in what came to be called a deathless realm, a sensuous heaven with form.

Sinha did not age. Each day blended with the next. Without purpose, without family, he isolated himself.

The noble asura continued to fear him, labelling him a killer and a defeater of tyrants and demons.

*In truth, I did what was asked of me. The Greater Gods created me to be the key to solving the riddle. Mahishasura had hobbled himself long before I arrived.*

Thinking the asura might fear him less, Sinha spent years looking for a way to transform back into a cat. Lord Shukra, the wisest asura teacher, laughed for days. He told Sinha to meditate. That he wasn't the first nor would he be the last—asura-man-animal hybrid. Yet, he was the only one in the immortal realm.

Sinha returned to the place where he had last seen Channa alive. He sat with his back to a mountain above a cliff, a sheer drop at his feet. The wind roared, pushing his whiskers and mane back.

The bull-headed god had landscaped the fabric of the immortal world. How had he been so blind to his power? There were none among the asura who could move mountains. Why had he become Hiranyakshipu's first minister when he had the love of a wife and a herd to serve? He had spent millennia in service to his people—how could he throw all that away, and for what?

Sinha would give up his invincibility in an instant if he could belong. He had given up on making friends. He held no affinity with the increasingly hierarchical asura who were ruled by indulgence. He missed the warm connection, grit, and unpredictable nature of humans.

He recalled the last night he had shared a meal with Channa's mother. The older woman had doted on him as she refilled his plate. He had not known what he was eating. He had not shared a meal since Channa's death. The asura had no value or need for food.

His eyes watered. Where were *they* that night? Sometimes, the time between births was long. Being born as a human was rare. Oumo had been a hunter. His subsequent life had been that of the hunted: a rabbit, a deer, a moose. Oumo had been born, again and again, until he wasn't.

He saw neither Saida nor Channa's rebirths.

Banchic died an old man and the leader of his tribe. He was reborn as his grandson. Sinha watched the boy grow up and be chosen as the leader of a much larger tribe. Watching Banchic's lives sustained his loneliness.

The night sky was vacant. The landscape below was shrouded in darkness. Far away from the asura cities, the world was still.

Sinha sat, brooding, "Now, what? I have completed my life's purpose."

In the dawn, the sun chased the shadows over the landscape below. A sudden rush of wind served as a warning. He heard the gravelly voice of Lord Ishwara: "You have proven yourself, Sinha. My gratitude comes late." The voice echoed against the mountain at his back.

A ray of light, a spotlight, shone where he sat. He felt a brief rush of wind sweeping upward. The cold air chilled his bare cheeks. He touched a face with smooth hands bearing razor-sharp claws. His palms touched bare skin, human ears, cheeks, brows, a human nose, moustached lips, and a beard.

"I am human?" he asked.

"You are asura," the voice replied.

"Is this meant to be a gift?" Sinha's face felt cold. He missed his fur.

"You have served well. What Hiranyakshipu lost is your gain. As you have discovered, you are invincible. His riddle now applies to you."

"Wait—I would prefer to be a cat," Sinha said. "Can I choose?"

"You never were a cat," the voice thundered.

"I was," Sinha whispered in stubbornness born of frustration.

"You are a lion. You are the King of All Animals."

"I did not ask to be a king or a lion. I don't want to be a god." Sinha hammered his right fist with his left hand.

"You became divine when the mortals began to worship you, Sinha. You protected and liberated the enslaved. Their descendants do not forget you. By your actions, you became a god."

"I don't—"

"It is in you to be both man and lion," came the voice's cryptic response.

"Who would welcome a lion at their hearth?" he persisted. "I liked being a cat."

## A Lion's Head

"You are a lion. Find a hearth that welcomes a man."

"I don't want to be a man," Sinha said. "Lord Ishwara, can't I ever be a cat again?"

There was no answer.

He sat with his back to the cliff. For the first time, he felt cold, inside and out. He sat shivering. His fingers ended with the wickedly exaggerated claws of a lion. "What am I to do with these?" he sighed. "How do I even transform?"

He thought of his warm, comforting mane and felt the transformation in an instant, like slipping into a warm pool of water. As a lion, he sat upright, his back to the cliff. At least in this form, he did not feel cold.

# Epilogue

It took the six years after the fall of Hiranyakshipu, for a small village of freedmen to build a small shrine dedicated to Narasinha at the foothills of the snow-covered Himava Mountains. The builders would take their stories with them when they departed for the mortal realm. Since then, shrines for Lords Sakka, Ishwara, and Surya came to have carvings, statues, or paintings depicting Narasinha's defeat of Hiranyakshipu.

He began as their god's champion. He would become the god who protects. Some would later claim, "he is an avatar of the universe." With stories passed down from father to son, mother to daughter, long after the last descendant of Prahlada's dynasty had turned to ash, temples were being built in worship of Lord Narasinha.

**SINHA'S STORY CONTINUES IN . . .**

# A LION'S PRIDE

# 1

**AFTER ONE THOUSAND YEARS ASLEEP...**

"Sinha?"

Sinha awakened and tried to open a single eyelid, cringing at the bright sunlight and startled by the dull crack of something breaking. He shuddered, but his muscles were locked and his body stiff.

Why was it so hard to open his eyes? He rose stiffly on all fours and shook himself. Plaster made from sand, lime, and water broke into clumps or crumbled to dust and flew in all directions as he moved.

Was it a side effect of sleep? Had he been asleep for a year?

The young sapling that had sheltered him when he lay down had grown tall and wide. Its canopy stretched to shade the entire courtyard in dappled sunlight. Several years, then. The tree brought the memory of the temple garden of his creation and its single baobab tree.

There had been as much light, accompanied by the uncomfortable compression of having been squeezed into the small body of a house cat. This was not that compression.

## A Lion's Head

He was in his lion form, though movement proved painfully stiff. He flicked his tail and stretched, releasing another cloud of lime dust.

Transforming into a man, he felt his limbs stretch, his furry body grew smooth, releasing the last of the coating from his body. This transformation left him dressed in simple garments: unbleached cotton trousers and a tunic. His hair, the same auburn of his lion form mane and tail tuft, tumbled down past his shoulders. His fingers ended in cruel, talon-like claws that marked him as an asura, a demi-god.

Sinha knelt to examine a piece of the fallen plaster. With admiration, he ran his clawed finger along the painted lines of fur.

"A side-effect of falling asleep for a thousand years, old friend."

Sinha whistled.

"Is that normal?" he asked.

"It happens," the Greater God, Sakka, replied. The infinite cosmic energy of the universe chose to appear as a priest with silver dreadlocks gathered in a topknot, a long white beard reaching his bare navel, and a white dhoti wrapped around his waist.

"The beard is new," Sinha observed.

"I am trying something different. Thank you for noticing."

"Is there another war? Have you come to give me purpose?" Sinha asked. Next to him was a long-forgotten shrine bearing the petrified offerings of flowers and fruit. He looked at the rubble in wonder. The immortal realm did not decay. How was it crumbling?

"There is always another war, Sinha, but that is not your concern—this time," Sakka replied with a smile. "You belong in the mortal realm." The god chuckled. "We created this realm to entrap the invincible asura who sought to destroy the universe."

"I intend to serve the universe."

"Yes, and you completed your service when the asura Hiranyakshipu passed to the next life."

Sakka began walking up a mountain trail. Sinha followed, picking his way through the increasingly rugged terrain as Lord Sakka continued. "The universe expanded, I think, perhaps, to fit all of our stubborn egos. There is room for all. We adapt. We change."

"If you say so."

"A riddle for you, Sinha: the lives of humans are a mirror to all life. I trust you to find its meaning. Make a study of humans and time. Time, I suspect, is not linear." Sakka used his index finger to draw a line in the air. "I have lived through three ages, each has been exponentially shorter than the last." He marked three consecutively shorter lengths. "I have felt for a time that, although the universe expands, the pace of time quickens. For once, I worry about what is to come next. Fewer years pass in each age."

The lines vanished. Sakka drew a newborn baby. "Rebirth as a human is rare. They are born ignorant of their karma and are ruled by it, yet they have free will." The form of the baby evolved into that of a child, a youth, and an adult. The outline of the adult human slowed, bending double, it crawled with deliberate weakness and finally lay prone before vanishing like dust in the wind. "Their lives pass in the blink of an eye. This riddle confounds me."

"Learn time and study humans—yes, Lord Sakka."

"Sinha?"

"Yes, My Lord?"

"While you are in the mortal realm,"—the corners of Sakka's mouth turned up—"perhaps you could learn to live a little?"

"If you wish it, My Lord." Despite Sinha's lingering grumpiness from having risen from sleep, the Greater God's belly laugh was infectious, and he cracked a begrudging smile.

The old man stopped before a smooth rock face. Engraved into the mountain was a circle crossed and divided with long, smooth lines and glyph markings—a stargate.

"You wouldn't believe how complex this thing is despite it looking like a child's drawing," Sakka said. He touched his fingers to the etched circle, and the engraving flared, outlined in a golden light. Multi-coloured glyphs soon appeared: blue, purple, green, orange.

Sakka hesitated. He held his index finger over the wavy blue lines for water, the orange peak for the earth, and the yellow star for the sky. "Need to get the timing right," he muttered. "Ah, there we go!"

All light and colour became absent from the stargate, replaced with a circular black portal that winked to reveal a scene: a blue sky and bright sunlight—the mirrored view of the mountain at their backs. "Do you see a difference?" Sakka asked with the pride of an architect.

Sinha could make out specks of birds flying in the distance. The hum of activity, from millions of creatures of every size inhabiting the mountain, filled his ears. The air smelled—alive. In contrast, the immortal realm had been sterile and silent.

"There is abundance," Sinha observed.

"Not always," Sakka cautioned.

"Do mortal lions become men like me?"

"No, you are unique. But, as far as big cats go, you will find lions are also unique."

"Curious," Sinha said.

Sinha stepped across the threshold. The soft ground was teeming with organisms, yet his foot did little to affect them.

"You will grow accustomed to your new surroundings." Sakka traced his fingertips lightly across Sinha's forehead. "You have done much service. Go with my blessings."

Sinha took one last look at the god and smiled. Happiness and hope welled in his heart for the first time since Channa had died.

"You will find humans are different from when you last encountered them," the god warned.

Sinha did not mind. Perhaps his companions from that long-ago past had been reborn. Soon after his creation, the gods had blessed him with three human companions: Oumo, the elder; Saida, the warrior; and Banchic, the young man. While helping Sinha to defeat Hiranyakshipu, Oumo and Saida had perished. The trauma of witnessing their deaths had led Banchic to fear all asura, including Sinha, who had borne the face of a lion and the body of a man. After completing his quest, Sinha befriended Channa, another human who had once served under the water buffalo god-turned-demon Mahishasura.

Thinking of Channa brought to mind the beaded necklace at his neck. He still wore it—the cure to Mahishasura's curse.

A sapling of the tree of knowledge, planted in Sinha's mind at his creation, had matured in the thousand years he had slept. Sinha was aware of the continuous expansion of the universe since his creation. Realms expanded and overlapped or split over time, resulting in a greater separation between gods and men. Asura—considered demi-gods, monsters, or minor demons—were scattered throughout the known universe. There was no likelihood of encountering the demon Mahishasura in the mortal realm.

---

Captivated by his new surroundings, Sinha did not register Sakka waving a last farewell on the other side. The portal closed behind him.

"Go, Sinha. You have been our pawn for too long. It is time for you to walk your own path." The god form of infinite cosmic energy smiled. "May you be happy and free."

---

### Sinha's journey continues in

### A LION'S PRIDE

Available in paperback and eBook formats.

## About the Author

Diliny M. De Alwis is a Canadian-born Sri Lankan author, living just north of Toronto, with her large family of three kids and three pets, who often serve as inspiration for her books. Her passion for researching and writing prehistoric fantasy grew while playing pachinko through several careers. When not writing, she can be found volunteering for the cadet corps and teaching.

## Enjoy this book?

Help others find A LION'S HEAD by leaving a review on StoryGraph, Goodreads, Amazon, or wherever you buy books.

Better yet . . . tell a friend.

## Thank you!

Printed in Dunstable, United Kingdom